THE HOUSE OF THE SEVEN FLIES

Victor Canning's first novel, *Mr Finchley Discovers His England*, was published in 1934, since when he has been a full-time author with over thirty novels to his credit. He is also the author of many short stories and serials which have been published in the principal newspapers and magazines of England and America. Born in Plymouth in 1911, he was a features writer for the *Daily Mail* before the Second World War, during which he was commissioned in the Royal Artillery. He has worked as a scriptwriter in Hollywood and now lives in Andover. His recent novels include *The Python Project*, *The Melting Man*, *Queen's Pawn* and *The Great Affair*.

THE HOUSE OF THE
SEVEN FLIES

VICTOR CANNING

UNABRIDGED

PAN BOOKS LTD : LONDON

First published 1952 by Hodder & Stoughton Ltd
Republished 1970 by William Heinemann Ltd
This edition published 1973 by Pan Books Ltd,
33 Tothill Street, London SW1

ISBN 0 330 23597 4

To
the captain and mate
of
Cora

*Printed and Bound in England by
Hazell Watson & Viney Ltd,
Aylesbury, Bucks*

NOVEMBER 1944

Kapitan Walter Maserling put the list in the pocket of his greatcoat. He stood in the doorway of the wooden hut and between him and the dim lights of the waiting car he saw the slant of the cold night rain break and whirl as a gust of east wind whipped across the yard.

The sailor at the wheel of the car, seeing him move forward down the duck-boarding, tossed his cigarette away. Maserling looked up at the sky. It was starless and possessed by the wild calling of the wind. A second sailor opened the rear door of the car for him and he dropped back against the damp leather upholstery, shrugging himself down into the darkness of his coat. He grunted an order.

The car moved off, the wheels skidding a little in the mud of the yard. As they crossed the dock bridge and entered the town he heard the beat of a church clock mark the half-hour after midnight.

The car felt its way through the dark streets. Shut up inside the houses there were people who would hear it, and know well what car was still abroad after curfew ... How the Dutch hate us, he thought.

The car stopped at the entrance to a small square. As the engine was shut off he heard the fat assault of rain-water on the canvas top.

He got out and the two naval ratings stood with him on the pavement. A flight of narrow steps ran up to a black doorway. One of the men switched on a hand torch and the rays picked out the running beads of water that slid along the curves of the ornamental work flanking the steps.

Maserling nodded towards the door and the two men climbed the steps. He followed them. The torchlight wavered on the door for a moment, seeking the keyhole and, in its unsteady haze, a brass plate made a sudden blaze of light. Across the plate were the words *Nieuwe Hollandse Bank*.

The heavy key was turned in the lock and the door swung inwards. They were in a tiled hallway, sombre with heavy furniture and obscure portraits in dull gold frames. Two tiny combs of gas-light wavered and spurted in the draught about a candelabra set high in the shadows of the hall. Maserling pushed the door close behind him and the light steadied slowly.

A man sat in a chair placed in the angle made by a wood and glass partition that crossed the hall. He stirred, his eyes blinking slowly, and a newspaper slid from his knees to rustle across the tiles. He stood up.

The sailor who had driven the car drew a revolver from his pocket. He raised it, aiming carefully and shot the man. The watchman dropped back against the partition and, his leg bending up under him, the steel plate on the heel of one of his boots made a long screech as it scraped across the tiles.

Maserling opened the door in the partition. The two men followed him. They went through the small counting-room, across the square back hall and down a flight of steps. At the bottom of the steps was a strong-room door.

Maserling pulled the folded paper from his pocket. While his two men watched he set the combinations on the three dial faces. When he had finished the men took each a lever and put their weight on them. The door opened and an automatic light came on inside the strong-room.

Maserling motioned the men inside and stood himself at the doorway with the paper in his hand. He began to call names and numbers from his list. From inside the room his men brought and stacked outside the door the personal security boxes he named.

There were ten boxes in all, and he could tell by the way his men lifted and carried them that they were not heavy.

One of the sailors tipped a long steel deed-box free of old, red-taped files. Maserling lit himself a cigarette as the men broke open the security boxes and packed their contents into the deed-box.

They lifted the deed-box and he followed them. In the front hall the watchman was doubled up grotesquely like some of the old men he had seen dozing uncomfortably in the crowded corridors of night trains. There was no blood to be seen; a quick, neat, uncomplaining moment of death. The ruthlessness of killing the old man wakened the beginning of anger in him. He fought it, remembering his official instructions : 'Leave no alien witnesses'. Official instructions, orders, the old man a cipher to be wiped out, and himself an obedient automaton . . . He moved on quickly after his men.

He slammed the outer door behind him and held the torch for the men as, the box between them, they went down the steps.

'Willemsdorp,' Maserling said, when he was in the car, and then added, 'It is permitted to smoke.'

They went south from Dordrecht. The steady rain made a bamboo curtain before them. Above the note of the motor Maserling listened, almost without being aware that he listened, for the higher note of another motor. But tonight the sky was empty of threat. There was only the rain and the wind.

Entering Willemsdorp they cut down to sidelights. They bumped down to a small landing stage. A man came forward from the head of the water steps. It was a sailor in oilskins, the tails of his cap ribbons flapping across his cheek in the wind.

'Kapitan Maserling?'

'Ja.'

Maserling got out and one of his men carried the deed-box down the steps to a waiting motor launch. In the bows another sailor in oilskins stood beside a spandau mounted on a low tripod.

The box was put in the cabin. Maserling dismissed his men who returned to the car. The launch moved out from the landing stage and swung down the canal towards the head of the Hollandsch Diep. Maserling sat in the lee of the cabin, a foot between him and the man at the wheel. The machine-gunner snugged himself down into a recess in the deck behind the gun.

'You know these waters at night?'

'Ja, captain. Like my hand. From here and up the Haringvliet to Hellevoetsluis.'

'Why the spandau?'

The man at his side laughed.

'There has been trouble lately, captain. You hear the *chug chug* of a boat and then the lead begins to fly about your ears . . . the boys in clogs are getting very brave. They do not like us.' The man laughed again as though the whole thing were a joke and the Dutch incomprehensible madcaps.

'How long shall we be?'

'Three hours, maybe a little less. We have the tide with us. And in this . . .' a broad hand slapped the curve of the wheel, 'we do not have to stay in the channels. She draws little water.'

There was more wind than rain now, and little patches of the sky were clearing to show the stars. Occasionally the dark loom of a buoy moved past them and he could see the curded edge of disturbed water where the racing tide kicked against the tilted shape. Once they ran in close to the shore and he saw a light flash and heard the sound, clear and sustained on the wind, of a cock crowing.

'Willemstad,' said the man at the wheel.

They swept on through the darkness and he began to doze, lulled by the sound of the motor and the soft passage of night shadows.

When he awoke the motor had been shut off and they were drifting silently on the tide. The man at the wheel, seeing him stir, lifted a hand warningly and nodded ahead into the darkness. He sat there, listening, but there were no sounds except his own breathing, the gentle sigh of water running under the stern and the whistle of the wind which had turned much colder. He saw the man forward swing the spandau and half-rise to settle himself firmly behind the gun.

Directly on their port quarter a light came on, a great white beam that for a moment blinded him. He heard the beat of a marine engine, an angry froth of water and then the ugly broken rattle of a machine-gun. He saw the spandau swing and then, as the light went out, saw the smooth tails of tiny flame from the barrel mouth against the darkness.

Across the water and darkness someone shouted, derisive and excited, and the light probed back at them from another quarter. He saw the man with the spandau begin to turn, and then the launch was suddenly full of a vicious swarm of bullets. He heard the bite and snap of lead against wood and metal, saw the white-edged flail of splinters and heard the man forward cry out with a soft, final desperation in his voice. The light went. A marine motor roared somewhere around them and the darkness was full once more of angry noises as a heavy-calibre machine-gun chattered. Something hit him in the arm and he was thrust backwards as though the darkness itself had struck him. He fell sideways onto the cockpit boards. The gun out in the darkness gave a last jabbering howl and, as he dropped into unconsciousness, he felt the launch shudder and heel against the sweeping shock of steel.

He came back to find himself staring up at a sky which was just beginning to lighten into a dirty grey pall. He lay there listening to the swirl and run of the water which had risen high in the bottom of the boat. He was shivering continuously and was weak from loss of blood.

Slowly he pulled himself up. The launch was drifting on the easing tide and ten yards away on the starboard hand he saw the grey of land fringed with a stiff barrier of reeds and a sloping rim of sand bank. The launch was low in the water and listing. He stepped forward and fell against the cabin door which swung forward away from him and brought him stumbling almost to his knees. He dragged himself up and saw that the foredeck by the spandau gun was deserted, the gun swinging loosely on its tripod with each movement he made. He glanced behind him and saw the dark outline of a sailor's body awash with water aft of the wheel.

9

The land moved by with a slow, fantastic precision, its shapes growing clearer each moment.

He watched the water rising rapidly and knew that soon it would top the freeboard and the launch would sink. He moved, touched by a sudden anxiety, and struggled to ease himself from his greatcoat. As he dropped it and leaned forward to rest himself, breathing heavily, he saw the deed-box in the cabin. Water reached almost to its lid.

The boat lurched and he heard the eager sound of water surging inboard. The launch began to settle. It went down under him, swaying and tilting for a while as the tide swirled over the gunwales. He was left to thrust his way weakly towards the shore.

Time abandoned him. He was aware only of a blackness of pain and weakness in his mind. Now and again the morning leapt back at him, striking against his eyes with a sharp intensity. He was in the reeds, his body wet and muddy. He moved and stumbled through blackness.

He opened his eyes and the morning light assaulted him, making his body shrink with the brutality of the sudden blaze. He lay with loose gravel under his hands. Before him as he raised his head, he saw a black, unsteady pattern. He stared at it stupidly for a while and then saw that it was an ornamental gateway worked with a thin tracery of wrought-iron flowers. Scattered among the flowers, stiff and archaic in outline, were seven flies, black and ponderous. He lay there and, as darkness swept over him once more, he heard the clump of footsteps moving down the gravel beyond the gate.

CHAPTER ONE

Under water, the light was a cool, jade green, alive with a yellow mottling from the morning sunlight. Furse could see the rope twisted tightly round the blades and shaft of the *Arletta*'s propeller. He would have to cut it free, and he was a man who hated cutting good hemp. He let his breath ease out gently, knowing he was good for thirty seconds. As he worked with his knife, he cursed the boys who had snarled the rope up like this . . . but there was nothing harsh behind his anger. He had a boy of his own.

He came up and reached for the *Arletta*'s rudder post, hanging there, breathing hard, the severed rope-ends and his knife in one hand. The fair hair was drawn down over his broad, brown forehead in a wet fringe. About his neck and shoulders the water glistened over the firm muscles.

A Customs officer came to the dockside, looking hot and overburdened in his heavy serge uniform. As he stared down, Furse gave him a quick grin.

'Damn boys got my dinghy painter fouled round the propeller.' The voice was lazy and pleasant.

The officer held up an envelope, a pale splash of colour against his dark suit.

'Telegram for you. They asked me at the hotel to let you have it as I came by.'

'Thanks. I'll be up.'

Furse shook his hair from his eyes and began to swim round the *Arletta*'s counter. He swung himself up a rope ladder hanging over the side. The water ran from his big, heavily muscled body, making dark pools on the pale deckboards.

As the Customs officer handed him the telegram, he was thinking almost enviously of Furse. That was the life; live in a boat and earn your living from it; no ties; no responsibilities: free as a bird; not even a wife to nag him.

Furse opened the telegram unhurriedly. It was addressed to Edward Furse, Yacht *Arletta*, Little Ships Hotel, Felixstowe Docks, and read, 'Coming this afternoon. Isaak Sluiter.'

Furse was relieved. For a moment he had wondered if he was going to lose a charter. Fifty pounds was important to him.

'Not bad news, I hope?'

Furse smiled and shook his head.

'No – just a charter party who wants to start a day earlier.'

'Going foreign?'

Furse twisted up the telegram and tossed it into the water. He knew what was behind that question.

'No. Not this trip.'

The officer nodded and wished – since he liked Furse – that he could say frankly that it would be wise if he confined himself always to innocent trips. He had seen the reports on Furse . . . but, even so, it was not easy to write him off as the usual type that ran into trouble over smuggling. Ex-army officer, architect or something like that before the war, busted marriage . . . just enough private means to keep him unsettled, but somehow not at heart unscrupulous enough to take this kind of life without regrets . . . there was a boy somewhere, too. One day he would slip up – and then they would get him. He hoped it would never come to that.

'Where are you going?'

Furse shrugged his shoulders. 'Mucking around the estuaries. Maybe we'll run up to Bawdsey for the night. Wherever he wants to go. It's his money.'

'Who is he?'

'Sluiter's the name. Don't know him from Adam.'

When the officer had gone, Furse went below to dress and have lunch. He came on deck later, a big, easy-moving man in his late thirties, his hands in the pockets of his old flannels, the sun laying a bright sheen on his damp hair, the blue of his shirt heightening the blue of his eyes which were frank in the firm, half-smiling face. Dropping to the quayside, he sat on a pile of timber to wait for Isaak Sluiter. Originally the man had planned to come the following afternoon. A fifty-pound charter. Fifty pounds . . . he could do with it. He had a boy of fourteen to keep at school. There were other parties booked for later in the summer, but even so things were going to be tight . . . He pushed the thought of money away from him with a sudden impatience. What was the good of worrying about it? He and Jimmy would get by somehow.

A sparrow flew down from the chocolate and brown ferry station building and began to take a dust-bath at his feet. He shut his eyes. The air was full of sounds, the rattle of a winch from a tanker on the far side of the dock basin, the regular thud of sacks coming off the end of the chute at the milling warehouse, the cry of gulls and children's voices, and the faint drone of an aeroplane coming in from the sea. He dozed in a pleasant haze of thoughts until he heard the motor of a taxi coming down the road to the ferry station.

The taxi drew up and a man got out and reached inside for his luggage.

Furse watched him and knew that this was his man. His interest in him, he thought, was almost non-existent. Two weeks of mud-work and fine-weather sailing for little more than would cover a month's school fees for the boy and a few cigarettes and whiskies for himself. And there were twelve months in a year, and one year followed another, and he was thirty-five and the boy fourteen and the letters that came from his bank about his overdraft he often never opened for a week. It was in that moment that he decided that he would write to Charlie Ponz in Rotterdam and take him up on his last offer.

The sparrow, feathering at his feet, flew away and a pair of highly polished, pointed black shoes took its place.

'Mr Furse of the *Arletta*?' It was a precise, strong but foreign voice.

Furse stood up.

'That's me.'

'Sluiter. Isaak Sluiter.' He stood there, a suit-case in one hand and a leather brief-case under his arm.

The man smiled at him through rimless glasses. Furse gave him a nod and reached out for the suit-case, his eyes going over Sluiter. The pointed shoes, the long, unusually lean body with its dark suit, the white face with its pouchy eyes . . . the tight sucker mouth . . . there was nothing there that pleased the eye, but he held back any judgement, allowing himself only a wry awareness that he was due to spend two weeks with the man.

'I'll make some tea and, if it's all right with you, we'll move off afterwards. With the tide we'll make Bawdsey tonight.'

'Good.' Sluiter stood there and Furse saw his eyes go over the *Arletta*. 'What was she? Pilot cutter?'

'Yes. Danish. I picked her up for a song some years ago.'

'I like the look of her.'

'She's steady, if you don't press her. Built to get there, not to race there.' Furse kept the affection from his voice.

Sluiter looked back along the quay, a jerky, uncertain movement, and murmured absently, 'Yes . . .'

He saw Sluiter's eyes pass from one group to another of the people on the quayside waiting for the next steamer, an alert, anxious scanning of faces, and Furse felt that the man was on edge, might even be afraid.

'You waiting for someone else?'

'Eh? No.' Sluiter's eyes were on him speculatively for a moment and Furse saw the corners of his mouth twitch, and he realized the man's pallor came from fatigue or illness. 'Let's go aboard,' Sluiter said suddenly.

Furse took him below and gave him the double-bunked fore-cabin. They had tea and then, while Sluiter went forward to change, Furse took her out into the estuary on the motor. When Sluiter came up he had changed into a blue sweater, grey trousers and deck shoes. Furse gave him the wheel while he went forward and hoisted the jib and mainsail. Furse came back and switched off the motor and he saw from the way that Sluiter was handling her that he knew what he was about. He had that tiny pang of jealousy which always hit him when he saw someone take her and make her move easily, knowing the hands on her were right.

Sluiter gave him a smile as he joined him.

'She is good.'

Furse nodded. 'This isn't the first time you've handled a boat?'

'I am Dutch, Mr Furse. All good Dutchmen learn to handle boats.'

Outside the wind was just east of south and the sea and tide were sluicing down with it. The *Arletta* was running fairly free towards Bawdsey Ferry. Furse took over the wheel and handed Sluiter the glasses so that he could look at the Cork lightship away on their starboard.

'You know Holland?' Sluiter said it quietly, the glasses up to his face.

'Yes.'

'Speak the language?'

'Yes. I was there during the war, and since.' Furse was a little wary. This man was not making conversation. He was reaching for some point.

'You can handle this boat alone?' The glasses came down and Sluiter turned to him.

'Yes. Between us it'll be easy. But if you like I can pick up a hand at Bawdsey. There's no need for you to crew.'

Sluiter was silent as he pulled a case from his pocket and ducked his head behind the wheel guard to light a short, fat cigar. The blue smoke eddied about Furse in lazy whorls and then was whipped away by the wind.

Sluiter spoke through his teeth, biting gently on the cigar. 'I don't want to go to Bawdsey.'

'It's your money. Where do you want to go?'

'Holland.'

Furse was silent. Over the port bow the tall radio masts at Bawdsey pitched and tossed gently above the thick line of firs and the sea raced past them in formal, white-tipped crests as well behaved as the rollers in a child's drawing. He said slowly, 'You chartered me for a two-week trip along the

East Coast. Fifty pounds. Now you want to go across the North Sea?'

'That's right.'

'And back?'

'No.'

'You had this in mind when you chartered me?'

Sluiter hesitated, then nodded.

Furse sucked at his lower lip, wondering how far he could go with this man, wondering how much he wanted to reach Holland.

'You said you'd seen my advertisement in *The Times*. Who put you on to me?'

Sluiter was smiling now, a prim, old-maidish expression.

'A man in Rotterdam. He said you were reliable. That is my opinion, too.'

'Charlie?'

'Yes.'

'I see.' He reached for a cigarette. 'What are you taking in?' he said.

'Nothing.'

'What do the police, here or over there, want you for?'

Sluiter laughed drily. 'Nothing. If the Customs cutter comes out you don't have to avoid it. My passport's in order. Here it is—' He made a movement to his hip-pocket.

Furse stopped him. 'Don't bother. Where do you want to go?'

'You have charts of Holland?'

'The whole lot.'

'I want to go to Veere. Then you are free. With decent weather you could be back in England under the week.'

'Meaning?'

'You get two weeks' charter money for, say, five days' work.'

Furse laughed and shook his head. 'For fifty pounds you could have hired a private plane to Holland – if you're so anxious to travel without company. That's it, isn't it?'

Sluiter's lips tightened over the end of his cigar. He said sharply, 'I dislike flying.'

Furse leaned forward and hauled the jib sheet home tauter and, as he straightened up, he said, 'I don't think so. Your suit-case is covered in KLM stickers. Some of 'em pretty new. However, let that go. If this wind lasts we could be in the Roompot in twelve hours. But—' He broke off deliberately. He had the advantage and he meant to ride it hard.

'Money?'

'What else? I'll take your word for it that you're not up to anything, but I've got to have a cash guarantee.'

'How much?'

'The charter money now. And then another fifty, in guilders or dollars or anything you like.'

'Another fifty?' Sluiter shook his head. 'I'm not a rich man, Mr Furse. Another twenty, maybe.'

Furse smiled. 'You want something, you must pay for it. Fifty.'

Sluiter stood up and moved carefully towards the hatchway.

'All right. I'll give you the fifty now. For the rest you will take my cheque?'

'Certainly.'

Sluiter went below and returned after a while. He handed over fifty one-pound notes and a cheque. Furse counted the money and then put it with the cheque in his pocket. Putting the helm down he began to haul in the main sheet as the *Arletta* from running free wore round and headed east.

The *Arletta* was shouldering her way with a firm grace through the sea. As she threw up her bows and rolled a little, there was a sharp, quarrelsome smack of water against her white counter. From the darkness which surrounded the pale binnacle light came the steady voices which keep a ship company at sea, the finger-tapping of a halliard against the mast, the groan of a block, the steady whip of a lashing hitched to a deck stanchion, the ceaseless hiss of the sea sliding away under the stern and the long, varying cadences of the wind slurring across the mainsail. Somewhere astern

17

of them the loom of the Galloper light cartwheeled faintly. It was nearly three o'clock and the short June night would soon be gone. The compass swung gently under the lubber-line between a hundred and a hundred-and-ten. Furse took his hands off the wheel and lit a cigarette. The *Arletta* was sailing herself. With this wind it was going to be an easy crossing.

Furse sat there thinking about Sluiter. Since before midnight the man had been lying on his bunk forward seasick. After supper Sluiter had taken the watch until ten o'clock and when Furse had come up to relieve him he had found the man obviously ill. He had helped him below, given him a shot of whisky and left him covered with a blanket.

He wondered why the man wanted to go back to Holland this way. He might get it from Charlie later. Now he was going over he would run up to Rotterdam and see Charlie . . . Unless something turned up soon he had a feeling that next spring might see him back at a drawing-board and the *Arletta* sold to some swine in a yachting cap and nicely pressed trousers . . .

He got up and went to the hatchway. He stood for a moment with his hands on the top of the sliding cover, feeling the gentle tremble of the *Arletta*. At the masthead the long burgee was beginning to be visible against the lightening sepia wash of the sky. With morning, he thought, the wind might back a bit. He went down to see how Sluiter was doing.

The man was lying on his bunk in shirt and trousers, the blanket on the floor.

'Anything I can get for you?' Furse touched him on the shoulder.

Sluiter half-opened his eyes and stared at him as though he were having difficulty in focusing. Then his eyes closed sleepily.

'I'll get you a drink.'

The man had been vomiting into the bucket Furse had left him and the fore-cabin was filled with the nauseating odour of sickness. Furse brought him a drink, but Sluiter refused to be roused. He lay there with his eyes closed, breathing faintly. Furse decided to leave him alone. Seasickness took people differently. Sluiter was obviously the kind who asked for no more than to be left undisturbed in his misery.

Furse went back into the main cabin and poured himself a drink. He sat down and wrote up his log. The *Arletta* was sailing herself and, when he had finished, he gave himself half an hour's sleep. They were well off the steamship lines and there was no danger. When he woke he glanced in at Sluiter. He lay there, still and miserable. Furse went back to the cabin. Through the hatch he could see the wheel and the sky beyond was now a pearl wash. He went up and saw that the dawn was coming through, dead ahead. He stood there, forgetting Sluiter, wishing that he had Jimmy with him. This was the kind of moment to feel yourself young and alive . . . Jimmy would enjoy this. This summer he would bring him across, give him his first long trip and let him share the exhilaration of a fine dawn, out here in the open, far from the stink and muddle of the land.

Much later when he went down to see if Sluiter was feeling like breakfast, the face that looked up at him from the bunk told him quite clearly that here was someone who would never breakfast again.

Furse slipped his hand under the man's shirt. The man was dead. Under his fingers, against the flesh, he felt the hard line of a small key which hung on a cord about the man's neck.

He pulled a blanket over Sluiter and went back to the wheel. There was no point, he thought, in turning back. They were more than half-way across and Sluiter, anyhow, was Dutch, and the cheque was drawn on a Dutch bank. There might be delays in getting it through. It would be more convenient if he were on the spot.

He lashed the wheel and went below. He made himself coffee and ate a few biscuits. Then he went forward and began to tidy up, unsurprised by the instinct for neatness at this moment. He had known it so often in the Army.

He straightened Sluiter out, rolled the blanket tightly round him and over his face, and then whipped a couple of lashings across the bunk to keep him from rolling out. He opened the ports and the forward deck-hatch to freshen the place up. The man's clothes, his suit-case and the brief-case were in the net rack above the bunk. He took them down and remembering the man's need to return to Holland this way, he went through his clothes. There was little of interest in them, a cigar cutter, matches, a wallet with some Dutch and English money, a penknife and a fountain-pen. In the suitcase were Sluiter's clean clothes. At the bottom of the case was a thin, black cardboard box. Inside was a hypodermic syringe, two narrow bottles filled with capsules and a small carton of ampoules, three of which had been used. As far as he could see Sluiter had nothing hidden. He picked up the brief-case. It was locked. He debated with himself for a while. Taking the body in was going to stir up a turmoil of regulations. To find he had brought in something illegal would put him in a bad position. He slipped the blanket off the body and took the key from Sluiter's neck.

He went into the main cabin and sat down at the table. He unlocked the case. Inside was a slim file of correspondence in Dutch and German, marked *Nieuwe Hollandse Bank*; a well-worn His Majesty's Stationery Office publication, Treaty Series No 56 (1947), entitled *Agreement on Reparation from Germany, on the Establishment of an Inter-Allied Reparation Agency and on the Restitution of Monetary Gold, Paris, January 14th, 1946*, and a long foolscap manilla envelope which crinkled as he fingered it.

Methodically he began to go through the file, finding that his Dutch and German carried him easily. As he read his interest rose. The file began with a copy of an old report of the Allied Agency detailing the facts of an official German raid on the Nieuwe Hollandse Bank on the night of November 2nd, 1944, when the watchman was shot and ten security boxes rifled. The Bank, apparently, had been much used by Amsterdam diamond merchants and most of the boxes contained uncut stones. The contents of the boxes were listed, and the valuation of the stolen stones was given as nearly a quarter of a million pounds. From the moment the raiders had left the bank no trace of them had ever been found, and their identity had never been established. Thereafter came reports and letters detailing the efforts made to trace the stones and quite a few of the reports were signed by Sluiter, who apparently had worked for the Agency.

Fifteen minutes later Furse leaned back against his bunk, pushing the file from him, and lit a cigarette. The hand holding the cigarette shook with a fine tremble. He stared at the coloured spines of the books in the rack on the far side of the cabin, he heard the quiet strain and bicker of the *Arletta*'s gear above him, felt the sway of the cabin and automatically braced a foot against the table stanchion . . .

Anyone seeing him in that moment could not have divined the sudden ache of new excitement which was striking at him; a big, fair-haired man, his face solemn and half-pensive, slumped back in an attitude of careless relaxation, long fingers pulling gently at his lower lip. Sluiter had traced a Kapitan Walter Maserling to his death and had found out that a quarter of a million pounds worth of precious stones lay somewhere in a stretch of the River Maas known as the Haringvliet . . . It was a part of the river Furse had sailed many times.

His eyes went to the unopened envelope on the table. He stirred suddenly. A quarter of a million. Waiting to be picked up if a man had the courage, the nerve.

He opened the envelope. Inside, tightly folded, was a well-creased but unmarked British Admiralty Chart, Number 192, *of the Rivers Maas and East Scheldte, Haringvliet Brouwershaven and Roompot to Hollandsch Diep*. He knew it well. There was a similar chart in his own rack. Pinned to the corner of the chart was a six-inch square of blue tracing-paper. On it were three crosses irregularly spaced. Under the centre cross were written the words *Zeven vliegen* and a little to the left of this cross was a dotted circle the size of a small nailhead. He examined the chart carefully.

It was simple, he thought. All a man would have to do

would be to find some landmark near the Haringvliet known as *Zeven vliegen* – that was Dutch for 'seven flies' – and then fix it on Chart 192. The overlay would do the rest. Since it had not been necessary to name the other crosses it could be assumed they stood for landmarks, churches or buoys already marked on the chart. Orient the overlay – and the little dotted circle would show where a quarter of a million lay . . . He straightened up, aware that his hands were trembling.

No, he couldn't do it, he decided abruptly. The stuff belonged to a bank, and beyond the bank, to men and women . . . smuggling was one thing – but this would be stealing. But would it? Insurance and Allied reparations had covered any loss. It was easy not to think about other people, especially when one's own need was so great. Here was a fortune waiting to be picked up . . . money which would set him and Jimmy up for life. There was risk in it, but he had taken risks before, and he knew enough about himself to realize, even while he argued with himself, that he was going to do it. He was suddenly hard and determined. A man had to look after himself and his own these days.

He took the chart and the top two letters off the file of correspondence and went on deck. Without these the documents in the case gave no clue to the whereabouts of the stones. Deliberately, taking his time, he tore the letters and chart into small pieces and dropped them astern. The pieces eddied and whirled as he released them, slipping away like a cloud of small butterflies to be swallowed up by the creamy wake of the *Arletta*. It was done, he thought. He could not handle it right through alone, he thought. He would have to have Charlie later on, but to begin with it would be better to keep as much as he could to himself. Charlie was his friend . . . but to friendship, especially with a man like Charlie, there was always a limit.

He went below and replaced the file of correspondence and the pamphlet in the brief-case, locked it, put the case with the rest of Sluiter's stuff in the rack, and returned the key to Sluiter's neck.

Back in the main cabin he lifted the mattress off his bunk

and took up the duck-boards to expose one of the long, galvanized water-tanks. It was a riveted tank, painted grey. With a screw-driver he prised up four rivet heads along the top edge of the forward panel. The rivet shanks came out easily, well oiled, and Furse slid off the end panel to reveal a false compartment about a foot wide and the full depth of the tank. Inside lay an old German Luger and a box of ammunition. He slipped the blue overlay inside the manilla envelope and dropped that in with the revolver. Replacing the panel and the rivets, he gave the rivet heads a quick lick of grey paint where the screwdriver had scratched them.

When he went on deck it was to find that the wind had veered to the west and the *Arletta* was off her course. He brought her back and now, running almost dead before the wind, laid a course which he hoped in a few hours would bring him to the Meerwerk buoy at the head of the Roompot off Walcheren Island. With the morning there had risen a slight mist and he knew there was no hope of picking up the flat Dutch coast until he was well in.

CHAPTER TWO

The haze stayed with him until after midday. From time to time as he ran along the edge of Walcheren Island he got a glimpse of the rising sand-dunes and the grey plugs of the old German fortifications. As he reached the mouth of the river to run up to Veere, the haze lifted and he saw away upstream the tall, moorish-like carillon tower of the town. The wind dropped to an idle breeze and, the tide coming downstream against him, he started the motor. He went up slowly against the strong current, the sails shaking and complaining loosely, his eyes watching the black port-hand buoys that swam down on the brown flood towards him. It was a tricky channel and, although he knew it well, he gave it all his attention.

He was a little way below the town when he saw a small rowboat slide out of the harbour entrance and race down on the stream towards him. Once the rower looked round, rested on the oars and raised an arm in greeting. He paid little attention. He was not going into the harbour. It was full of fishing-boats and was a noisy resting-place. He meant to turn into the lock cut above the town and lie up beyond the lock in the canal which ran through to Middelburg. But as the rowboat dropped downstream he saw that it was making for him. With his foot he eased down the throttle until the *Arletta* was just breasting the tide and making hardly any progress.

The rowboat slid abeam of him and then swung round. The water boiled from lusty oar strokes and then the boat was alongside him and a pair of hands had grasped the *Arletta*'s gunwale and a rope was tossed inboard. It was a manoeuvre which was done skilfully and not learned in five minutes.

'Hullo there!' It was a warm, pleasant voice, the accent behind the English words slight.

'Hullo to you,' he said, and then added with a smile, 'be careful of my paint there.'

'Don't worry. I will not scratch your beautiful boat.' For the moment there was a teasing quality in the voice as though the girl who stood in the rowboat, her body braced against her hands on the *Arletta*'s rail to keep her craft away from its side, understood the homage paid to fresh paint, clean decks and tidily stowed gear.

She stood there, holding her boat off from the *Arletta*, and her short-cropped dark hair was tousled forward over her brown forehead in attractive confusion. About her neck she wore a red silk scarf, the ends flapping up into her face in the faint breeze, and the bracing of her body brought her young breasts up, full and firm against the soft wool of the loose grey sweater which, he noticed, was darned and stained with oil. No lipstick, no nail varnish, he thought. For all that, she knows what she looks like, and likes the picture . . .

He stretched down a hand to her.

'You'd better come aboard. It'll save you rowing back against the tide.'

He took her hand and hauled her up and she gave a kick of her foot that set the rowing-boat drifting astern to be caught up on the painter he had made fast to the *Arletta*. She came up and, unsteady for a moment, swayed against him. He put out an arm and held her, his fingers cupped against her shoulder. He held her, experimentally, for a second or two longer than was necessary and, as she moved away, he thought he saw a shadow of amusement pass across her face as though it were an experience she was well used to and could easily deal with.

'Did you have a good crossing?'

She was beside him at the wheel now as the *Arletta*, the motor roused by his foot, plugged up abreast of the town.

'Fair.'

'Where's Mr Sluiter? Down below?' As she spoke she began to move towards the companion-way. Furse put out a hand and stopped her.

'How did you know I had Mr Sluiter aboard?' He made no attempt to hide his surprise.

'You have, haven't you? This is the *Arletta*, British—' she nodded towards the red ensign at the stern.

'You came out to meet Mr Sluiter?'

She gave him a laugh. 'Of course. He sent me a telegram saying he was coming. Why do you look so surprised?'

This was the beginning, he thought, and he had to go carefully. Already, from this pause, he felt that she had caught the change of feeling which had taken him,

'He's aboard,' he said quietly. The lock entrance above the town was coming up on the starboard hand now, but he let the *Arletta* run on. 'Do you mind before you do that—' he put out his hand to keep her at the wheel by him as she made a movement forward '—if I ask you a question? It's rather important.'

'Go ahead.' He could see she was puzzled now.

'Is Mr Sluiter any relation of yours?'

She shook her head. 'No. My name's Straatsma. Constanta Straatsma. I know Mr Sluiter, but only in a . . . a business way.'

The hesitation was clear and he wondered what lay behind it. He could feel himself cautious and alert. What did she mean? In a business way . . . For a moment he almost asked her. No. His line was to wait and let things come to him.

'Is something wrong?' she asked.

The girl was watching him. She liked the look of him, big, capable and with a friendly smile.

'Yes, something is wrong. I'm afraid you'd better not go below.'

'Why not? I want to see Mr Sluiter.'

'I'm afraid you can't. I'm not being tiresome. I'm just trying to find the right way to go about things and it isn't too easy. You see, Mr Sluiter is dead—'

'What?' It was as though someone had struck her. She stood there, staring at him.

26

'He's dead,' he said gently. 'He died on the crossing.'

After a while she said, 'He can't be dead. How could he be dead . . .' It was the voice of a small girl, lost and feeling the presence of closing shadows.

'I'm sorry.' Then as she made no move, he went on, knowing that action can salve distress, 'I'm going about. Perhaps you'd like to take the wheel and run us into the lock entrance. I'll get the sails off her.'

She nodded, but said nothing. He moved away as she took the wheel. From the foot of the mast he looked back and called, 'You feel up to it?' He stood there with his hand on the main halliard and she looked up.

'I'm all right,' she said. 'I'll take you in.'

Furse enjoyed the drive in the bus to Middelburg. He knew Holland well enough not to be surprised at the effect it had on him. The flatness and neatness of the country never failed at first to dull the imagination. It was a country which seemed to offer nothing except an unexciting conformity of scene and movement, a series of flat cardboard cut-outs childishly arranged. But after a while, he began to acknowledge the persuasive deception of his first impression. It was like a painting by Avercamp or Steen : the closer you examined it the more you saw, the more excited you became at the constant discoveries of human comedy and colour . . . The little houses with their crow-stepped and baroque gables, the brightly painted shutters, the clean toffee-look of the cobbled streets, the yellow and green geometry of the fields, ruled with the indigo lines of ditches and canals, the cumbersome cartwheeling of a windmill's vanes, the flash of gold from a woman's head-dress, the tight black velveteen jacket of an old man, round fur cap on his head and a cluster of pearls brooched at his throat, and the melon, red and bone-white clogs, slowly all began to warm and refresh the imagination.

He sat in the bus, wedged between a fat farm-wife, fantastically neat and starched so that as she breathed her clothes emitted gentle explosions, and a young lad in stiff

Sunday clothes who was on his way to Flushing for his medical examination for military service. They talked across him, begging his pardon for their impoliteness with friendly smiles. He sat back, hearing them but his mind engaged on the turmoil of the afternoon of the previous day.

The girl – Constanta; a nice name – knew her way about a boat. She had brought him into the lock, helped him warp through and had been very useful with the Customs officials and the police doctor who had eventually arrived from Middelburg. She had disappeared before the body had been taken ashore through a curious little crowd which had gathered on the canal bank. By the time he had finished his statement from the *wachtmeester* – the chief constable – at Veere it was late evening. Returning from the town to his boat, he had found the lock-keeper waiting for him with a message asking him to call at the Middelburg police head-quarters the following morning.

He sat in the bus, wondering where the girl had gone, and what her business with Sluiter had been. Perhaps he would see her in Middelburg. He hoped he would, and smiled to himself at the easy way she had slipped from him when he had held her too long.

In Middelburg he found the police building and was taken to a room which looked out at the copper-sheathed roof of the cathedral. The room smelt of varnish and waxed leather and the floor was tiled in blue and white squares. Someone had heeled a cigarette stub on the tiles by the desk. It lay there like an obscenity in this quiet, spotlessly clean room.

Normally, waiting about was not a process which irked Furse. But this morning it did. In destroying some of Sluiter's papers he had taken a definite step. Now, when the police began to question him, he had the choice of taking another, and he was by no means fool enough not to know that it is step by step a man is drawn into the complicated web of deceit and wrong-doing. At this moment he was free to withdraw . . . a little unpleasantness and it would all be over . . . You've got to go on, he told himself. It's a chance

28

that only happens once. If you can make no bones about smuggling, why hesitate at this?

In the next room to Furse, a room almost identical in furniture and fittings, sat Herman Molenaar, assistant detective-inspector from the Rotterdam Police Headquarters. On the desk in front of him was Sluiter's brief-case and a small file of papers.

Molenaar, too, was a man who did not mind waiting. His whole life had taught him the value of patience and waiting. If you were patient and waited long enough, he was convinced, then things happened and difficulties dissolved. He had waited ten years to achieve his present position. He had waited five years for his wife to agree to marry him. He had waited for criminals to make a loose remark or a careless movement. All these things had happened in their time, and he was now convinced that time was an ally of the virtuous and persevering. It also, he was shrewdly aware, made up for certain defects of intelligence and insight in himself. He knew he would never be a brilliant policeman, but he was sure he was a thorough one.

He rang the bell for Furse to be shown in to him.

When Furse entered Molenaar nodded to the empty chair by the desk and said pleasantly :

'I hope it was not inconvenient for you to come here this morning, Mr Furse?'

'Not at all.'

'You speak Dutch?'

Furse smiled and said, 'Well, I maltreat it a bit, but most people seem to understand it. '

'Good. We speak Dutch then. After a few little phrases my English is not so good.' Molenaar put his hand out and squared the brief-case in line with his blotter. It was a nice smile, he was thinking. Oh yes, a nice, pleasant Englishman; fair hair, blue eyes, a face that took the lines of a smile easily, cornering the eyes with sun-wrinkles. The girls would like him, he thought. Careless about his dress, but then you don't come off a boat you've brought over single-handed looking like a bandbox. He said nothing for a moment, waiting and watching Furse. He felt that he detected a slight nervousness in the man.

'My name is Molenaar. Herman Molenaar. I am not of the Middleburg police. I am *adjunct inspecteur* of the *Hoofbureau van Politie* in Rotterdam.' He went on, anticipating Furse's inquiry. 'Mr Sluiter was a resident of Rotterdam and – in view of certain circumstances – the police here felt we should be called in. I have read your statement, but I am hoping we shall get a little more help from you.'

'Anything I can do.' Furse watched him, watched himself, caution strong in him as he wondered why a man from Rotterdam should have been called in. This was the beginning of the skirmishing, but if he handled himself right there was no danger for him. This man, Molenaar, did not look dangerous. He was tall, about Furse's own age, and with a healthy bulkiness which suggested a farmer rather than an assistant inspector from Rotterdam Police Headquarters. There was no suggestion of subtlety about him. The grey suit was well cut, the blue silk shirt showed, perhaps, a little too much cuff and the tie was a shade too bright for this building. Furse suspected a touch of vanity in the man. When he smiled his broad face became a warm caricature of bluffness, with a kind of Toby jug healthiness and good nature.

'How exactly did Mr Sluiter come to charter your boat?'

'He answered an advertisement of mine in the London *Times.*'

'To cruise, I think—' Molenaar ruffled through his papers —'in English waters?'

'Yes. But he changed his mind as I've already stated.'

'Did that seem curious to you?'

'Naturally, but he offered to pay me extra so I decided to bring him across.'

'And no questions asked?'

Furse smiled to himself. In the dry tone of his words Molenaar had revealed himself. This was a policeman, shrewd, patient, and taking nothing on trust. Furse began to like him.

'He paid me an extra fifty pounds.' He took out his wallet and slipped Sluiter's cheque across the desk to Molenaar. 'I have to make a living, Mynheer Molenaar. Do you think this cheque will be honoured?'

Molenaar put the cheque on top of his papers, ruffling its edge with a finger and thumb. 'Leave it with me. I'll see it gets passed on to the executors. It may be a little while, but eventually you will get your money. Tell me, Mr Furse – you admit that you were curious at Sluiter's change of mind. Didn't your curiosity lead you to anything else?'

'Such as?'

'Well, when I'm curious, I make up little theories to satisfy my curiosity.'

'You mean, did I wonder why Sluiter wanted to come back to Holland in such an odd way?'

Molenaar nodded and came round and sat on the edge of the desk.

'Exactly.'

'I had a vague feeling that he was suddenly anxious to leave England.'

'Ah, so . . .' The last vowel was drawn out. Molenaar sat there rubbing a broad hand across his chin and swinging one leg. The length of sock that showed now, Furse noted, was in the same mood as the tie, just a little too fancy. He was suddenly conscious of his own socks which were ex-Army grey, and wrinkled down to his shoe tops.

'Go on, Mr Furse. Why did you think that?'

'I don't know. Nothing definite. Just his manner, the way he talked. I think he was frightened and trying not to show it.'

'That is what I want, Mr Furse. Often when one runs out of facts, it is helpful to have impressions, the odd feeling. You know what I mean?'

Molenaar hoped he sounded convincing. He was not interested in what he himself was saying. He knew that if Furse were innocently involved in this affair and had

31

anything definite to say about Sluiter it would have been already said. But was the man hiding anything? He was far from ready to commit himself to any opinion yet on that . . . one had to wait.

Furse stood up. Some things you could not miss, and this was one. He went to the window and stood there with his hands in his pockets. Then he said slowly, 'I think I would be able to cooperate more if you were frank with me, Mynheer Molenaar.'

Molenaar made a low humming noise in his throat and came forward to the window, beaming. 'You are very quick, Mr Furse. I like that.'

'What was Sluiter up to?'

'Nothing, as far as I know, Mr Furse. He had a small marine insurance broking office in Rotterdam and he was in England on business. If he felt like it there was no reason why he should not come back to this country on your boat, the . . .'

'*Arletta.*'

'Yes. The *Arletta.*' Molenaar pulled a cigarette case from his pocket and held it out to Furse. 'You know, your impression was right. Sluiter was afraid – of somebody.'

Furse shook his head at the cigarette-case. 'I felt he was.'

Molenaar gave him a disappointed look. 'You do not fully understand yet?'

'No.'

'A pity. It means, I'm afraid, that I shan't get much help from you. Isaak Sluiter did not die a natural death. He was murdered.'

'How could he have been?' Furse turned quickly. 'There were only the two of us on the boat.'

Molenaar's face was lined with a serious, reflective look. 'Don't misunderstand me, Mr Furse, but one of the hardest tasks in my profession is to judge when the surprise in a man's voice is genuine. I think you are genuinely surprised.'

'You're damned right I am! I don't even believe it!'

'It is true. Sluiter was murdered. He was a diabetes subject and we have ascertained from his doctor in Rotterdam that, although he carried a hypodermic syringe and insulin capsules, he took insulin generally once a day in solid form. Without insulin he couldn't live. Taking too much, also, is fatal.' Molenaar lifted a paper from his folder. 'I won't bother you with the full autopsy report, but Sluiter died from an overdose of protamine zinc insulin taken at about ten o'clock in the morning of the day he joined you. The bottles in his case should have held capsules of ten units per cubic centigram. Someone had exchanged them for 100-unit capsules. His being seasick and vomiting his food enhanced the effect of a pzi overdose causing him to go into a—' he glanced at the paper in his hand, '—hypoglycaemic coma twelve hours after the dose, and eight hours after this he was dead. Everything you've told us of his behaviour substantiates this. Sluiter was murdered – unless he chose a particularly unpleasant and odd way of committing suicide.'

'If he meant to commit suicide why ask me to bring him across? Death is the same whichever side of the North Sea you take it aboard.'

'So, too, I think, Mr Furse. Whoever planned his death knew quite a lot about medicine and about Sluiter and his habits.' Molenaar went back to his desk. He shook his head lugubriously. 'It is a very sad business, and awkward for you, too, to be mixed up in it. Such a nuisance. However, we will try to make it as least trying as possible for you. You know Holland?'

'I fought over part of it during the war, and I've been here a few times since.'

'Then you will not feel too lost if I ask you to stay in the country for a few days until this business has been regulated?'

'Have I to stay at Veere all the time?'

'No. You can move about as you like, of course. We can find you, if we want you for the official inquiry. Tell me, did you go through Sluiter's luggage?'

'I packed up the stuff he had lying around.' Furse knew his voice sounded casual, too casual perhaps. Ought he to have shown a touch of anger at the mild but deliberate

33

emphasis on the word 'through'? Maybe not; anger was not a privilege ordinary citizens allowed themselves with the police in a foreign country.

'I see. When he came aboard in England, he had just his suit-case and a brief-case?'

'That's all I saw.'

'You didn't open the brief-case when you were packing his other things?'

Furse gave a little laugh. 'What would you have done, Mynheer Molenaar? A man comes aboard for a cruise, then pays me extra money to take him to Holland, and then dies on me. I'm like anyone else; I like to know what I'm handling. I packed his suit-case and had a good look through it. I'd have done the same with the brief-case, but I couldn't find the key.'

Molenaar chuckled and then rose. He put his hand on Furse's arm as he led him to the door.

'Thank you for being so honest, Mr Furse. I had a little wager with myself that you would admit to your curiosity. I should have done the same in your place.'

Furse paused at the door. 'Where was the key?'

'On a thong round Sluiter's neck, Mr Furse.'

'Ah, I didn't think of that.' He was silent for a moment and then added, 'Tell me, there was a girl called Straatsma who came out to meet my boat at Veere. She said Sluiter had sent her a wire to meet him. You know about her?'

'Certainly, Mr Furse. We know all about her. Mejuffrouw Straatsma is the proprietor of the Straatsma Sleepdienst Company – that's a small tug-boat concern – and Sluiter was making inquiries for her in England about spare marine engine parts.'

'She can't help you about his death?'

'No. I am afraid not. Good day, Mr Furse, and thank you for coming. You have been very helpful.'

When Furse had gone Molenaar went back to the desk. He sat there for some time leafing through his file of papers. Then he leaned back in his chair and let his eyes wander to the slopes of the cathedral roof. In the bright June sunlight, the verdigris patina shone like the bloom on a greengage, and the grey and white pigeons courting on the stone ledges moved with a pompous, almost studied elegance that made him think of figures in a stately eighteenth-century dance. You could never be certain, he was thinking, never. Men and women were like cash accounts, from day to day you had to strike a balance and accept it. Only in the long run could you find whether they stood on the credit or debit side of truth. So far . . . this Furse seemed to be in credit. He thought of the man, picturing him as he had sat in the chair at the desk, lounging in it almost, his grey trousers creased from untidy packing, the old tweed jacket patched at the wrists and elbows, and that careless smile coming and going . . . a big, strong, healthy-looking man with a charming contempt, one would have thought, for detail and tidiness. But that was not true. He had shown an intelligent appreciation of the inflection in a word or phrase. An interesting character . . . it would be a pleasure, professionally, to work against him if he turned out to be a rogue.

He sighed gently and poised one finger over the bell-push on the desk. He would have to see the girl again. Now he had seen Furse it would help him with the girl . . . he hoped. He was well aware that he was not very good at dealing with women. Somewhere at the back of his mind was a persistent conventional distrust of the other sex. You never knew where you were with them, particularly the kind who came most into his office. When they were frank and open and engaged your confidence it was almost automatic that they were covering a dark and subtle intricacy of thought, and when it came to their own interests they could be ten times as ruthless as any man. He had been wrong about them often enough to know that here time and patience needed the third ally of constant suspicion.

When the police clerk showed Constanta Straatsma in and she was sitting before him, he had to make the deliberate effort not to be beguiled because she seemed a nice, straightforward young woman.

He said to her gently, his voice masking his own indecision

35

and uncertainty about her, framing it in fact with an almost avuncular concern, 'Mr Furse, I'm afraid, couldn't help me much. Are you sure you'd never heard Sluiter mention him?'

'Quite certain.'

'And you'd never heard of him before?'

'No. Sluiter sent me a telegram saying he was arriving at Veere aboard the *Arletta*. That was all. I went there to meet him . . .'

She did not add that she had gone there full of hope for that would only have stressed the disappointment she felt now. She was disappointed. She felt bad about it for in some horrible way it had dulled the shock of learning that Sluiter had been murdered.

Molenaar put the tips of his fingers together and stared at her over them. He went on solemnly, watching her and wondering about her. 'And you're quite sure that in these papers of Sluiter's there's nothing new, nothing which he didn't have or know when he left for England?'

'Absolutely. But he must have found out something else.'

'Why?'

She gave him a quick smile. 'I knew Sluiter. The fact that he sent me a telegram to meet him meant that he was excited and had something to tell me; meant, I'm sure, that his visit had been successful. How can there be any doubt of that? The fact that he has been murdered points to that as well.'

'Maybe.' It was odd, he thought, but for all he knew she and Furse might have planned the whole thing between them. 'As far as you are aware did anyone else know what you and Sluiter were after?'

'I never discussed it with anyone. About Sluiter I can't tell. I saw him very seldom and he had to make inquiries . . . Other people might have got to know.'

'It was rather an odd arrangement between you, wasn't it?' For the first time he let a little of his suspicion slip into the open and he saw her lips tighten at once, but he defended himself immediately with the reflection that any man who tries to trace truth in the expression of a woman's face is asking for trouble.

36

'I don't think so. During the two years after the war I was a secretary in his office at the Allied Agency and we both knew about the Nieuwe Hollandse Bank affair. Sluiter worked on it but never got anywhere. Then when I took over my father's business in Dordrecht, as I've told you, I came across a bundle of old German Naval signal messages in the attic of the office. That put me on to Kapitan Walter Maserling. I told Sluiter about it and we decided to go into the thing together for the sake of the reward offered by the Bank still. I put up a certain amount of money for Sluiter and he did the work.'

'You would have done better if you had taken your information to the authorities.' Any kind of private investigation was naturally disliked by him, but he kept his feeling out of his voice.

'But it was such a slim hope to begin with, and anyway we didn't want to have to share the reward.' She paused for a moment, considering Molenaar. Somehow she had the impression that it would be quite easy for her to dislike the man. He seemed (or was that just her imagination?) to be holding back from her and it suddenly occurred to her that he was probably far from sure of her own position in this affair. She said sharply, 'Anyway, the point is what do we do now?'

'We?' he smiled at her. 'You do nothing, Miss Straatsma. Go back to your business and wait. What there is to be done I can do. But I don't hold out much hope. The Englishman wasn't of much help to me, but we can make other inquiries.'

'What do you think about him? Do you think he knows anything? Could he perhaps have—?'

'Have murdered Sluiter?'

'Yes.'

'I don't think so. I can find out more about him, and for the time being keep an open mind. What was your impression of him?'

She was silent for a while, thinking about Furse. He'd

been considerate to her on the boat. A capable, pleasant man ...

'No,' she said suddenly, 'I don't think he has anything to do with this. He doesn't look like that.'

Molenaar smiled drily. 'They never do. However, when you go back to Veere you may run into him. I shouldn't try to avoid him, but if he talks to you let him talk. But don't tell him anything. He said that he tried to have a look inside Sluiter's brief-case but couldn't find the key—'

'He tried to do that?'

'Wouldn't you? After all Sluiter put rather an unexpected proposition to him and then died on his boat. No, he appears to have acted naturally enough. But the point is, if he's telling the truth then he doesn't know anything of the nature of Sluiter's business in England. If that is so, there's no need to enlighten him. If it isn't the truth – then he may make a slip and reveal something he's not supposed to know. All I want you to do, Miss Straatsma, is to keep your own counsel and look after yourself. Whoever murdered Sluiter will obviously have quite an interest in you. Does that worry you?'

Constanta stood up and shook her head. 'In the business I'm running you have to be able to look after yourself.'

'How is the business going?' he asked as he went to the door with her.

'Very well.' She spoke casually. It wasn't going well, simply because she hadn't enough money to do the things she wanted to do. It was odd. All her hope in Sluiter had been somehow centred on that. Her share of the reward would have put the business on its feet again.

'That's good,' Molenaar said, and his tone hid the fact that he knew quite well her business was heading for bankruptcy. She could have done with the reward. Was that all she was after? At the moment he did not know. He could only wait.

CHAPTER THREE

Furse had an hour to wait for his bus back to Veere. In one of the town hotels he found a cashier who – making a nice profit – changed twenty of his pound notes into guilders. After this he found a café in the main square and sat outside having a beer. He wrote a postcard to Jimmy. An old woman came up and begged half a guilder from him, and a man in clogs led a great Flemish mare, mane and tail bedecked with ribbons and plaited straw, across the square. Any other time he would have sat back, lazy in the sun and enjoyed himself, but today he could feel a stir of uneasiness inside him. He had known it before, chiefly when working with Charlie.

He was certain that he had given nothing away to Molenaar. That step had been taken. From now on, with luck, he would be left on his own. But the news that Sluiter had been murdered worried him. Somebody in England must have known how close Sluiter was getting, might even have known that the vital information had been uncovered and had made a bid for it. What more were they going to do now? They, or he, or she? People who used murder didn't give up easily . . . The whole affair was growing darker and his common sense hammered at him to get out, to quit now. But he could not. So far he was all right. Why should he give up a fortune because of a few fears? He could look after himself; the war years hadn't left him helpless when it came to guile and quick thinking. The war – not that he was the kind who blamed his own faults on the war – had bitched him up. Well, he had to take things as they came and stop feeling squeamish. The world was full of thieves. He had plenty of company.

He saw the girl, Constanta, come across the cobbles, a shopping bag swinging from her hand, and sit at one of the tables. She had not seen him. He was sure of that. And yet, at the back of his mind, he tried to undermine his own sureness. She might be pretending not to see him . . . Here we go, he thought. From now on he was going to be like a sea-anemone at half-tide, every tentacle alert, sifting, tasting, waiting, the whole organism ready to close tight at the first warning of trouble. She had a red and white striped skirt and a white blouse and she looked good enough for a magazine cover. The waiter brought her a coffee and a cream cake.

After a while Furse went over to her table. She gave him a little nod and the beginning of a smile.

'I've got some time to wait for my bus back to Veere. Do you mind if I join you? Say so if you do. I'm well trained.'

'Please do.'

'I would have come over before, but I thought it was better to let you finish your cake first. It looked the kind of job one prefers to tackle without company around.'

She smiled outright. 'I'm waiting for the Veere bus, too,' she said.

'You've been to see Mynheer Molenaar?'

'Yes.'

'Did he tell you . . . about Sluiter?'

'Yes. I don't understand it.'

'It's a bad business. Why on earth should anyone want to murder him?'

She shook her head. He could not know, she thought, to ask a question like that. It was said so naturally, sympathetically. Yet how could you tell?

At first Furse thought it was going to be hard work talking to her. She answered him, but to begin with never in any way which opened up any fresh lead in the conversation. He had to do that for himself. Gradually, however, she became easier, and he had the feeling that she was making a deliberate effort to put something from her mind, some problem with which she would rather have been left alone.

As they walked down to the bus together, he asked, 'Where did you learn your English?'

'I was at school in England for two years.'

'Did you like it over there?'

'No.'

'You don't like the English perhaps?'

Constanta smiled. 'Oh, I like them. But I didn't like school. I don't like being indoors.'

'An outdoor girl, eh? Is that why you run a tug company?'

'Who told you that?' The question had made her suspicious. She tried not to show it, but she knew that it was there, that no matter how casual and friendly this man might appear she must not forget that he had been with Sluiter and might know more than he had admitted to Molenaar.

'Molenaar told me. He said Sluiter was arranging about spare marine engine parts for you in England.'

'Yes.'

He took her arm and helped her up to the bus. It was crowded and they had to sit together. As he sat down beside her he said:

'Perhaps I'm asking too many questions. But we have been thrown together in an odd sort of way so that I don't feel we are strangers.'

He spoke frankly, and she was sure without any subtle undermeaning. She found it easy to like him. Perhaps a little ready to hold your elbow too long when he helped you on to a bus . . . but she did not mind that from him, and when he laughed it was a slow, lazy movement of sound that she found attractive. Of course he was untidy. His grey socks did not match and the pockets of his jacket bulged with odds and ends, and the handkerchief in his breast pocket had a smear of oil across one corner. Yet on his boat, she knew, everything would be ship-shape and a scratch on his paint would break his heart.

On the way back in the bus she told him that she had come down from Rotterdam in a small cabin cruiser which was now lying in the fishing cut at Veere. She was starting off for Rotterdam that afternoon. When he told her that he was going upriver, too, that afternoon and thought of spending the night at Zype or Dintelsaas, she recommended Dintelsaas to him, and not until he had left her realized that she had probably done so because she was often in and out of Dintelsaas with barges going up to the sugar-beet factory at Dinteloord. That was not, she argued with herself, because she just wanted to see him again, but because it could do no harm to keep some contact with him. She told him, too, where he could find her at Rotterdam if he got as far as that.

When they got out of the bus at Veere, Constanta found herself feeling that the journey had been too short. She liked him, liked his easy manner and more than once had found herself laughing in a way which had been quite foreign to her for a long time. It was the first time she had been so much in the company of one man for many months.

Furse left her with the promise that if he got as far as Rotterdam and had time he would look her up. He walked back to the lock, past the great Gothic mound of the cathedral. He stood for a moment on the wooden piles against which the *Arletta* was moored. She was a good boat, but she always looked a little clumsy when she was moored. When he had money, he'd keep her still, but he would have another boat, something with more line and speed . . . and he'd get a racing dinghy for Jimmy. They would have a house, too. Money . . . what a beautiful thing it was. As he stood looking down at the *Arletta*, he saw the water lap away in a series of gentle ripples from her side and he thought he heard the sound of movement come from the cabin. At once his dreams fell away from him.

He stepped quietly aboard and went to the companion-way, walking with caution. There was a man in the main cabin. He was slitting the cover of one of the bunk cushions with a jack-knife.

'It'll save you trouble and me expense if I tell you there's nothing in the cushions,' said Furse quietly in Dutch.

The man looked up in surprise. For a moment he was silent as though hesitating between some patent excuse or the truth.

'*Dank U, mynheer*,' he said. He dropped the cushion and

stood there with the knife in his hand. He was a trim, little man with black beady eyes and a rather sharp nose. He wore a brown suit and a bright red pullover and was, Furse thought, a bit like a robin, a perky but cautious robin, willing to be friendly but afraid to try.

'Close the knife and toss it up.'

The man hesitated, and looked at the knife and then at Furse. He closed the knife and tossed it up. Furse caught it and jerked it over his shoulder into the canal.

'Come on up.' Furse stood back.

Very slowly he came up and as he stood on deck one hand went to his face and the fingers tapped against his chin as though he were patting his smile into place, anxious that it should sit well and serve him properly.

'My apologies, mynheer. I did not expect you back so soon.'

'We don't have to be polite with one another. What's your name?'

'Dekker ... Anselm Dekker ...'

Furse saw his eye flick towards the wooden piles, gauging the distance from the deck.

He smiled. 'You'd never make it, Anselm. There are other things you should take into consideration, too. I'm five eleven and a half, and nearly a hundred and eighty pounds. You're about five eight and not an ounce over a hundred and thirty pounds. Also I don't think your name is Dekker.'

The man smiled. 'I thought you might think I was lying, mynheer. That is why I told the truth.' He pulled out his wallet and handed his identity card to Furse. It showed that he was Anselm Dekker. Furse handed it back.

'It's a good habit to cultivate. Let's see how long you can keep it up. What were you doing below?'

'Searching the place.' There was a faintly reproving tone in the voice now as though Dekker felt the question unworthy.

'For what?'

'Food or money.'

'I keep my money in my wallet and the food in the locker by the galley. What made you think there might be something in the cushions?'

'People hide their money in very odd places.'

'Who sent you aboard?'

'I came for money and food, mynheer. I have a wife and three children, a boy and two girls—'

'Oh, come off it, Dekker. You can do better than that. You'll be telling me next your wife has tuberculosis and one of your children is blind.'

'No, mynheer. My wife and family are in good health and well provided for.'

Furse realized that he would get no truthful answer to his questions. He spun the man round and grabbed him by the neck of his jacket and the loose seat of his trousers.

'On your way ashore, Dekker, you'd better have a look for your knife.'

He lifted him and pitched him overboard into the canal. Dekker went under with an untidy splash. When he came up, he blew water from his mouth, making a grimace of disgust. Then he looked up at Furse and said very slowly and with an emphasis which until then had been absent from his voice :

'*Jig rotzak!*'

Furse watched him swim awkwardly around the bows of the *Arletta* and pull himself onto the bank. He moved away, without a glance back at Furse, down the path towards Veere.

In the main cabin Furse found two cushions cut open and signs that Dekker had been through his lockers, his book rack and chart cases. Furse lifted the bunk cover and saw that the rivets on the water-tank were untouched.

There was the possibility that Dekker might have been telling the truth, but he doubted it. Sneak thieves were very rare in Holland, especially outside the big ports. Knowing now that Sluiter had been murdered and realizing, too, the incentive which might lie behind that murder, he was certain that Dekker had come aboard with the same thought in mind as Molenaar, to see whether he had in fact abstracted anything from Sluiter's brief-case. He knew what he had to do. The sooner he got to Rotterdam and saw Charlie, the better. He would not tell him everything – until he was certain of finding the stones. That was when he would really need Charlie.

He made himself a cup of tea, cut two large corned-beef sandwiches and, within half an hour, was taking the tide up the Zandcreek. Once out of the canal mouth into the river, he ran under sail, sitting comfortably at the wheel with his chart and a pair of field-glasses. There was not a lot of traffic on the river. A tug with a string of two dead barges behind came down the river and a great apple-cheeked sailing barge under motor and sail came tacking against the tide past him, the red sails spread like the wings of some huge bird.

At the mouth of the Zandcreek, when he turned into the Ooster Schelde, he had the tide against him. Furse watched again the familiar miracle of water, land and sky fusing so that windmills and church towers seemed to float in the unsteady glitter of the horizon. A ferry boat, coming across from Zierikzee, showed first as funnel and masts poised in the air and then, with a sudden click as though the eye had begun to function belatedly, revealed hull and the white comb of froth at her bows. In this country distance and light were the two magicians who made out a flatness a constantly varying beauty and delight.

Running up the Keeten Maasgat he was passed by Constanta Straatsma. The motor cruiser came up quickly behind him, then swung over and was throttled down to keep abreast of him for a while.

'When you get into Dintelsaas,' she shouted, 'tie up as close to the lock as you can get! You'll have enough water then to keep you off the mud at low tide!'

She gave him a wave of her hand, opened the throttle and was gone.

He came into Dintelsaas just as the light was going and berthed just below the lock. He turned in early and went off to sleep with the sound of calling sandpipers and curlew in his ears.

He was in Rotterdam by midday and booked himself a room in a cheap hotel near the station. The place smelled of cigars and caraway seeds and a glance into the dining-room convinced him that he would do better to eat outside. He got himself a meal in a cafeteria and then went to see Charlie.

Charlie Ponz lived in a flat overlooking the Rotterdam Park not far from the Royal Maas Yacht Club. Charlie was a South African – at least, that was as near as Furse had ever come to establishing his nationality. They had met in Italy, in an olive-crushing mill, just north of Arezzo. It had been an uncomfortable meeting and Furse had never discovered how Charlie – a medical orderly in the Union of South Africa Forces – had come to be present so far forward at a time when the Germans had decided to straighten out a bulge in their line. He suspected that Charlie had ventured too far in search of black market *vino, prosciutto* and anything else he could lay his hands on. They had spent four dangerous, but not unhappy, days in the mill and he had learned then all of any importance that he was ever to know about Charlie – that he could shoot straight, that he was as unscrupulous as he was brave, and that his friendship was real, even if given on the understanding that every man had his price and generally not a very high one. After they had been rescued they had met again in Naples, Florence and, finally, in Rotterdam where Charlie had put him in the way of a little business with the minimum of embarrassment to himself.

Charlie had a round, boyish face, sad, reproachful eyes and a manner that bordered perpetually on the verge of rising disappointment. He lived with his mother. Furse had never made any comment on the fact that each of the three times he had visited Charlie there had been a different mother – different in face, but the same in type; tall, well-built, well-dressed matronly women, always dark and possessed with the gift of silence.

Charlie's latest mother having served them with tea and little cakes, she disappeared. Charlie lit a cigarette, holding it awkwardly in his nicotine-stained fingers as though it were the first one he had ever smoked in his life, and curled his feet up under him in the armchair.

'Hell, this is a pleasure. What? But no surprise, sir. I know you are here the moment you spit on the stones at Veere. Private information, private wire. Expensive, but necessary in my business.' He held his cigarette up like a piece of chalk and frowned at it as though he had decided that as a pleasure it was over-rated. 'Now, you tell me, is this business or pleasure, or do I ask a damned fool question, sir?'

Charlie had never lost the habit of calling him 'sir', and his English was uncertain and unexpected.

'This is both, Charlie. But chiefly I want you to look after something for me.' Furse took an envelope from his pocket and held it up. Inside was the six-inch square of blue tracing-paper which he had taken from Sluiter's brief-case. 'Have you got a safe place?'

Charlie smiled and nodded. 'Leave it with me. You think much more or not at all about that proposition I make the last time?'

'I thought about it – but for the moment that's all.'

'That's what I guess, sir. *Verdamt!* I am saying to mother yesterday. You see, he'll be along. But not for my business. He comes in with a dead corpsus. We know that, eh? Now you tell me more and I go to work. Anything for you, sir.' Charlie got up and walked to the window, a squat figure in a wrinkled tussore suit. He fidgeted with the end of the window curtain restlessly, then turned quickly. 'No?'

Furse smiled. 'Your instinct's sound, Charlie – but you're going too fast. I just want you to look after this envelope for me. Later – I hope – I'll do a lot of explaining and shall want your help.'

'What's the percentage?'

'It might run as high as fifty.'

'You say that to other men, sir, and you are in trouble.

47

With me I won't hold you to your generosity.' He came over and took the envelope. 'It's sealed. When a thing is shut up like that, sir, I don't guarantee my curiosity won't get too strong.'

'You can open it now. It won't mean a thing to you.'

'In that case I leave it sealed. You sure you don't want help now?'

'I'm all right. Tell me – do you know a man called Anselm Dekker? A nice little chap who swims quite well and can't keep his hands off other people's property?'

'Maybe . . . *Inlichting, renseignements, informazione* . . . Can't run my business without it. I didn't know he was a swimmer.'

'Who does he work for?'

'Himself. Doesn't every man? But you pay him a hundred guilders and he works for anyone. He must be in a friendly mood to tell you his real name.'

'Friendly – and very sure of himself. What about Mynheer Herman Molenaar?'

'No, sir. You keep away from him. What he don't know – which is a lot – he is very good at guessing. Also he is patient like a monument.'

'And a girl called Constanta Straatsma?'

'You in trouble with a woman?'

'No. I got that over some time ago. Do you know this girl?'

'No.'

'That's the lot then. You hold on to that envelope and, maybe, in a few days I'll get in touch with you.'

Charlie came over and shook his head. His eyes were sad and for a moment his underlip trembled like that of a small boy who has been unjustly scolded. 'Major Furse, sir, that's not the lot. You don't ask me anything about a man called Sluiter who is dead on your boat.'

Furse stood up. 'Why should I, Charlie? I know you know him. You gave him a reference to me in England. But I know you can't tell me anything about him which would help.'

48

Charlie tapped his head. 'In here lot of stuff I don't put on the counter, sir. You try me.'

Furse went to the window. Outside he could see the massed trees in the park and beyond them the grey sweep of the Maas backed by wharfs and the rising trellis work of derricks. Momentarily he was tempted to tell Charlie everything, but some inner caution held him back.

'Why did Sluiter go to England?' He turned, watching Charlie.

Charlie shrugged his shoulders. 'You tell me.'

Furse shook his head. 'You see – you can't help yet. Later . . .' And then, because he liked Charlie, wanted to ease his disappointment and, maybe, lighten his own load a little, he went on, 'Do you ever handle jewellery?'

The dejection went from Charlie at once and the creases in the tussore suit seemed to smooth out as he squared himself up, alert and suspicious.

'You got to have the answer to that, sir?'

'Not if you don't want to tell me. All I want to know is could you . . . if?'

'Maybe I do it once or twice, but it is not my line. I stick to the river here . . . this beautiful, muddy Maas and all the lovely boats which come and go. Maybe, though, I do it sometimes.'

'Where? Antwerp?'

Charlie laughed, horrified. 'Antwerp – my jeepers, no! Anyone want trouble let them try Antwerp with that kind of stuff. You should know where I unload the last lot, I think. England.'

Furse stiffened. Suddenly the room was very still, poised outside time for a moment, fragmented into a scene which he seemed to be recalling from some old forgotten dream. 'What do you mean?'

Charlie flexed his lips into a wry pout. 'Don't you go getting angry now, sir. I just told you it was some stuff. I don't say it was all watches – but if you liked to believe that, OK, sir. It is better for us both.'

'Which trip was this, you damned old rogue!' Life was

moving again. It was no good, somewhere inside him the power to be angry with Charlie had long gone.

'The first one you did. It was with the watches. But don't worry, it is all finished with. I've got a bad habit of using my friends. With you I don't get used to that.'

'You ought to let people settle for themselves what risks they'll take.'

Charlie shook his head. 'No, sir. The first time a man does our kind of work he says he begins with a little risk, just to work into it. He's wrong. First time – take a big risk. That's when it's safest.'

CHAPTER FOUR

He really was enjoying the sun when Anselm Dekker came up to him. He gave him a half-smile rather than a frown simply because it was less effort. The paintwork of the seat overlooking the river was hot, comforting through his clothes to his skin. Out on the muddy tide a couple of boys were handling a tub of a rowing-boat, its bows patched in raw, unvarnished wood, with a dexterity which was pleasing to watch. Somewhere upstream a load of orange crates had been spilled over a ship's side and they were salvaging the water-logged boxes as they came racing down on the ebb. Both of them shouted with husky, slum-damped voices as they picked the boxes over the side.

Dekker squeezed himself on to the few inches of seat left beyond Furse's sprawling feet and began to roll himself a cigarette.

'How's the family?' Furse asked.

'Fine.' Dekker gave him a meek grin and shrugged his shoulders. He nipped the loose tobacco from the end of his cigarette and brought out a lighter, an expensive lighter with a little design of grapes and vine leaves in *cloisonné* on its sides.

'Where did you pick that up?' Furse asked.

'Off an American – he was very drunk. My wife . . .' Dekker puckered his mouth over the flame as he lit his cigarette, '. . . is very annoyed with you. The water has made my suit shrink.'

'You can hand it on to one of your boys.'

As he spoke Furse was considering the lack of surprise which Dekker's appearance had caused him. It was a development which he had expected, but half-hoped would not happen. He could meet Dekker banteringly, but his real mood was quite different. A man had been murdered in an unsuccessful attempt to take information from him. Furse now had that information. It was obvious that he must be a person of great interest to whoever had engineered Sluiter's death. It was an interest he did not welcome.

'The boss would like to see you,' said Dekker.

'That's what I thought when I saw you sit down. I don't want to see him, though.'

'You should come, though. He will only have to pay more money to have someone else persuade you. They would not be as polite as I am. I believe in politeness – up to a point.'

'I'm glad to hear it. I'll forget that you called me a bastard when I dropped you in the water.'

'The shock – for a moment I forgot myself.'

Furse rolled his feet off the bench and stood up. Don't think it's a joke, he told himself. That's how Dekker presents it, that's how I handle it, but both of us are really doing no more than put a polish on ugliness.

They walked slowly under the plane trees along the length of the Willemskade and then skirted around the Royal Maas Yacht haven. The tall masts of the berthed yachts reached up above the dark trees and the grey faces of the surrounding buildings, with a blinding ivory hardness, and he thought of the prosperous Rotterdam merchants who did most of their sailing over *schnapps* and large meals in the club restaurant. You could have gone anywhere in most of the yachts in the berth – and how many of them ever got their decks wet? It was like keeping a mistress and never visiting her. Money in the wrong hands. When this thing came off he would know what to do.

'In here.'

It was a block of flats overlooking the river. Plain freestone went up in a smooth run and over each window was a little canvas cockle shell of a canopy in striped colours.

There was a cool sweep of tiled hallway and then a lift about the size of a large coffin, highly varnished and with expensive fittings and a faint smell of eau-de-Cologne from the last passenger. Dekker stood in front of Furse, and he saw that on the centre of the man's head was a brown little patch of baldness as though someone had carelessly left a cigarette burning there some time. They stepped out on the fifth floor leaving the eau-de-Cologne laced with the smell of Dekker's close-cut tobacco.

'What's his name?' Furse asked.

'Ninus Rohner.'

Dekker spoke in a quiet, almost awed voice as though he were in church. The corridor had something to do with it. The lighting was bashful behind yellow frosted glass shaped like bishops' mitres and the thick carpet gave little gasps of indignation as they trod on it.

Dekker stopped at a door. He nipped off the burning tip of his cigarette into a sandbowl of heavy brass and stuck the dog-end in his breast-pocket.

They went in. The two people inside might have been posing for a photograph. Ninus Rohner stood by the window with his arm loosely round a woman's waist. He was a tall, boyish-looking man of forty, with a fresh complexion and a face which had an air of slight over-breeding. His eyes were pale blue and humorous. His hair was crisp with a faint touch of gold in it and he had a finely strung, restless body. Altogether he was a little too good-looking for any man to trust him. He wore his clothes, which were good, with a suggestion of carelessness which, Furse guessed, belied the thought he gave to them. He guessed further and decided that Ninus Rohner was a man who saw himself in the part of a frank, eager personality, anxious for all the world to be his friend.

'I'm glad you've come, Mr Furse. Won't you please sit down.' Rohner drew his arm away from the woman and waved to a chair. 'Elsa said you wouldn't come.'

Elsa was silent. She turned to a small table and poured some sherry into a glass. She was tall and dark with an expensive face that owed little of its attraction to nature. She came over to Furse carrying a glass and, with the movement of her body under the black cocktail dress, the poise of her arms and the way she walked, nature came back into its own.

'Sherry, Mr Furse?' It was a soft, friendly voice which for

a moment isolated the two of them. If they had been alone, Furse thought, it would have put him on his guard against himself.

'All right, Dekker.' Rohner gave the man a friendly nod which Furse was sure would make no impression on Dekker. He heard the door shut and in his imagination saw Dekker walk like a sidesman back to the lift, fishing for his dog-end in his breast-pocket.

'What do you want to see me about?' he asked.

'You are alone in Rotterdam. I thought you might welcome a little company.' Rohner's English and his accent were good.

'I like to choose my own company,' said Furse sharply. Somewhere over by the window he heard Elsa laugh gently and he saw Rohner's lips tighten so that they became mean and spoiled his smile.

'I thought we could straighten this out between us in a friendly way, Mr Furse.'

'Perhaps we're the wrong two people.'

Rohner caught the stubborn antagonism behind the words, understood the suspicion and strength in this man. He was being difficult. Very well . . . for the moment he could be patient.

'No. We're the only two people. And we understand one another. For the moment I'll concede that you are in a very strong position. By the way, what did you think of Mynheer Herman Molenaar?'

'He doesn't dress as well as you. His English isn't so good either. But I'd rather do business with him.'

Rohner stared shrewdly at Furse. 'If you'd any intention of doing business with Molenaar you would already have done it. You haven't, and you never will. That puts us into the same class. Sluiter's stuff was handed over to the police. But not all of it. You kept back certain things, Mr Furse. I don't blame you for keeping them back. I'm only annoyed that the opportunity came to you instead of me. However, this thing is too big for one man to handle. You must have realized that. Eventually you will need help. I'm offering to help you, Mr Furse, or – to make it simpler for you – to buy out your interest in this affair.'

Furse helped himself to a cigarette from a Delfware box on the table and Rohner held out a lighter to him. He knew that this was another step into the labyrinth . . . somewhere in the heart lay the prize. But should he go on? He could still return, go to Molenaar, or even keep his own counsel and go back to England . . . A quarter of a million, he told himself. Keep that thought clear.

'Well?' Rohner was waiting.

Furse looked round the flat. It was a triumph of bad taste over expense. The only thing he would have kept was a Van Huysum floral painting which needed cleaning badly.

Furse said, 'I've got a boy at an expensive public school. As he grows older his tastes and his professional training will be expensive, too. I want a house with some acres around it. I have a good boat, as Dekker has probably reported to you, but I'd like a better one. And that's only the beginning. Do you still think you can buy me out?'

Rohner laughed pleasantly. 'Let's forget that suggestion. It was made in the hope that you might prefer a quick, small profit and a minimum of risk. But we could still work together.'

'But why should I choose you as a partner?'

'Because I could make it damned awkward for you if you chose anyone else.'

Furse shook his head. 'I'm not looking for a partner.'

Rohner sighed and gave Elsa a quick glance as though he expected some sympathy from her over Furse's obtuseness.

'At the moment you are wasting your time, Ninus,' she said. 'I think you should give Mr Furse a chance to think it over.'

'I'm sure I can make Mr Furse see what a reasonable proposition it is.' He went to a door beyond the floral painting and opened it.

'Pieter!' he called.

Pieter came in. He had fair hair, a stupidly handsome face and friendly eyes. He was dressed in a striped vest and flannel trousers and could have made an easy living selling photographs of himself to health and strength magazines. Furse got the impression that if the man were not careful how he moved his enormous muscles would be thrown out of gear and he would trip up.

'Pieter,' said Rohner quietly as though addressing a child. 'This is Mr Furse. I want you to meet him because he may be working with us.'

Pieter dipped his head gravely.

'Ninus – you're being far too impatient.' Elsa came forward. 'You must give Mr Furse time to think it over.'

'I have thought it over.' Furse moved behind the table in the centre of the room. He did not trust the friendliness in Pieter's eyes. He moved to the door and Elsa came with him. No attempt was made to stop him from going.

When Furse had gone Elsa came back to Rohner. She stood before him, biting her lower lip gently.

'Well?' she asked.

Rohner shrugged his shoulders.

'I dislike the English, anyway. But to me he's just a stupid half-pay officer type. Hard-up, good in a fight. He had a bit of luck with Sluiter, and at the moment he thinks he can handle it. That won't last long. However, we'll play it carefully if you like.'

There was a telephone pay-box in the hall of Furse's hotel. He got on to Charlie and asked him about Rohner. Charlie knew him and disliked him. He was half-Dutch, half-French. His father – who had married a Dutch schoolmistress – had been a bank clerk in the Amsterdam branch of the Crédit Lyonnaise. Rohner had inherited all of his father's shrewd reverence for money and none of his honesty in acquiring it. As for Rohner's wife, Charlie did not know a lot about her except that he doubted whether she was married. Her real name was Elsa Lieven and, during the war, she had worked as a nurse in a military hospital. One thing he knew about her for certain – she could be twice as ruthless as Rohner.

56

'You listen, sir. You stay away from them. Damn, what kind of people you are meeting? Now I begin to get worried. You know how many bodies they pick out of the Maas each year? Not half as many that go in and never come up. Look, what the hell you do?'

'It's all right, Charlie. I don't need you yet.'

'If you're knowing Rohner, you need me. You find that out very quickly. How long you stay in Rotterdam?'

'I'm leaving tomorrow morning. My boat's down at Dintelsaas. I came up by train.'

Alone in the shabby hotel room he wondered why he did not pay his bill and get back to Dintelsaas that night. At the back of his mind he knew the answer. The girl Constanta had said she would be getting into Rotterdam that evening. He knew where her barge would tie up over on the other side of the river beyond the Kattendrecht quarter. He wanted to see her. He wasn't sure that he believed the story of machine parts from England. Rohner, Sluiter and this girl . . . did they all tie up together? He began to think of the file of papers he had gone through in Sluiter's case and of the little square of paper he had given Charlie. One of the letters he had torn up had referred to the 'Haringvliet project'. The Haringvliet was part of one of the mouths of the River Maas that flowed out to the North Sea and was flanked on one side by the islands of Overflakkee and Goeree and the other by Beierland and Vorne. He was not far from it at Dintelsaas, and somewhere in that stretch of water lay the answer to what he wanted.

The hotel proprietor, a fat, comfortable creature in a dirty shirt and alpaca jacket, came to his room and told him he was wanted on the telephone. He asked the man:

'Have you ever heard of a place called the Seven Flies?'

The man thought for a moment and then shook his head. 'No. There's a restaurant in Amsterdam called the Five Flies. Very famous. Seven Flies, no.'

It was Elsa on the telephone.

'I want to see you. It's important.'

'Where?'

'There's a dance hall called the Three Bridges, near the station. About eight o'clock tonight.'

The Driebruggen Club, Furse discovered, was a large sprawling wood and asbestos building. It had a couple of bars, a large dance hall and a small garden at the back hedged with long banks of thuya in tubs. At the far end of the hall, the orchestra was seated on three little bridges against a back-drop of yellow and green polder country, windmills and angular Friesian cows. The lighting was bad, the band indifferent and over the whole place hung a sad lethargy as though all present had long given up the preposterous pretence of enjoying themselves.

Furse seated himself in an angle of the hall and called a waiter.

He had just finished his drink when Elsa arrived. She gave him her hand as he rose and left it with him a shade longer than their relationship warranted.

She wore a green frock with a rather tight little coral necklace around her throat, a loose summer coat with large pockets, and she smelled expensive. He had the feeling that the better he got to know her the less he would trust her, but that had no effect on his liking her. It was the easiest thing in the world to like people without approving of them.

'If Ninus knew I were here there would be trouble.'

'I've a feeling there's going to be trouble anyway.'

'Not if you're sensible and clever.'

'You're setting me a high standard.'

She laughed, making a movement of her eyebrows which was attractive.

'Let's dance,' she said; 'I find it easier to talk that way.'

They went round the floor twice before a word was spoken. It was a long time since he had held a woman as closely as he was holding Elsa now. He liked the way she came into his shoulder and the way she moved with him. But, curiously, his thoughts took him to Constanta and he wished it was she he was dancing with, seeing in imagination the quick flush of her smile and the clean movement of her body. It was odd how she had kept coming into his mind.

'How well did you know Sluiter?' he asked Elsa.

'I'd met him once or twice. Ninus knew him. He was a dry old stick.'

'How did he know him?'

'They worked together for the Allies at one time.'

'You speak English very well.'

'Ninus – and some officers I knew during the war – taught me.'

'Ever been to England?'

Looking down he saw her smiling at him. 'No,' she said. 'But if you've a spare berth on the way back, I'll come with you.'

He took her round past a table full of solid citizens who were sweating over their *schnapps* and the effort of enjoying themselves.

'How did your husband come to know so much of Sluiter's business? I'm sorry so many of my questions begin with "How".'

She shrugged her shoulders, breaking gently from him at the edge of the floor and walking towards the doorway which led into the garden. 'I don't know. Also – he's not my husband.'

It was a warm night and the darkness of the shrub banked garden was accentuated by the glow of lights from the town.

'If he were, something tells me you would still be just as uninhibited.'

'It is a word I do not understand.' She was standing very close to him. It was a warm night and very dark. He thought, since there was going to be trouble, he ought to take what little comfort came with it. Yet even as he reached for her he knew that she had only stirred a hunger in him which she could not satisfy. In his mind it was someone else he was reaching to hold. He put his arms around her and she welcomed him with her mouth and her body. She would have kept it alive longer but he put her away and lit a cigarette for her.

'You can do better than that,' she said.

'Perhaps.'

59

'You kissed me as though you were thinking of someone else.'

'I'm sorry.'

'Never mind. You'll do better...'

'What do you really want with me?'

She was silent for a moment.

'You don't ever intend to work with Ninus, do you?' she said.

'No.'

'I knew it. When he realizes that, he'll be violent – and you can't go to the police. If you're clever, you and I can get over that. We can work together. You know why I'm talking to you like this?'

He laughed quietly, holding her by the elbows. 'I've got a theory but I'll keep it for a moment.'

'I like you. I think we could work together. You can't expect me to say more than that.'

They went back inside to their table and she opened her bag for her lipstick. Furse saw the edge of a dark-blue passport against the black leather lining.

'What do you suggest we do?' he asked.

She was silent for a while, arching her lips as she put her mouth back.

'You must tell Ninus you will work with him. Then, when the right moment comes... You and I...'

'I can fill in the rest of the story. When you get into the spare berth of mine where do you see us going?'

With a hard emphasis in her words as though a long deferred ambition had come within sight she said, 'Some place where the sun shines more than one day out of seven, where you can go for a drive and not be in sight of your own church tower all day, where a woman can lie back and relax in the right company – that's where I want to go.'

'You'll need a passport for that.' As he spoke he put out his hand and drew her handbag towards him. She made a half-movement to stop him and then thought better of it. He took out her passport and opened it.

'It's a very good photograph of you. But the name's different. I thought you were called Elsa Lieven?'

'I've got another at home with my real name in it. I find it useful to have two sometimes.'

'Naturally.' He flipped the pages over and then handed the passport to her.

'Tell me,' he said, 'how long were you a nurse?'

'A nurse?' She was surprised for a moment. Then she smiled. 'How did you know that?'

'It's not the occupation given in your passport – but I have other ways of picking up information.'

She was silent for a moment. Then she said, almost approvingly, 'Ninus has got you wrong, I can see that. You're going to give trouble – but not to me, not if we work together.'

He could see she was watching him, not afraid of him, but trying to move ahead and intercept his thoughts. Sluiter, he guessed, must have been easy for her to handle.

'I wonder how long *our* partnership would last?' he asked gently. 'Don't forget that Sluiter was murdered.'

'Yes, Ninus told me.'

'Sluiter was murdered because someone switched his insulin capsules. If it hadn't been for the fact that he changed his mind and came to me a day earlier than he had intended, he would have died in his hotel. You must have shown your hand too soon to make him change his mind.'

Her mouth was a dark score on the beautifully composed face. He went on, sure of himself, yet glad of the anonymous company which drank and danced around them. 'Someone had to be pretty close to Sluiter to be able to change his insulin. Very close. Closer than you and I have been so far. Do you want me to go on?'

'Why not? I don't blame you for thinking as you do. But you're quite wrong.'

'Sorry.' He stood up. 'You told me you'd never been to England. Your passport shows a British exit stamp for the same day that Sluiter came to me. I'd say you offered him the same terms as you've just offered me – and he was fool enough to take you with him. For a trained nurse the rest was easy. No, thank you. Go back to Ninus and tell him I'm not looking for a partner.'

As he moved away she said one word in Dutch. He had never heard it in his life before, but he had no doubt of the vituperation it expressed.

CHAPTER FIVE

It was a little before nine o'clock and he took a tram down to the Westplein by the river and began to walk up towards the Willems Bridge.

The tide was almost dead low and the Maas under the night sky was a great vein of reflection-shot malachite. Away to his left car lights streamed across the lofty iron Willems Bridge and along the far bank a chain of arc lamps patterned the darkness with stiff golden cones. Against the up-cast haze of light row after row of tall derricks stretched their angular necks like monstrous mechanical giraffes browsing on the smoke that hung over shipyards and refineries. Downstream a petrol waste valve flared from the edge of an oil depository, the red and blue flames twisting and swaying in the slight breeze.

He found himself thinking about Constanta Straatsma. After Elsa, the thought of her was pleasant, a contrast as forcible as coming out of a tunnel into the clean air and sunshine of a summer's day. She would be in Rotterdam now. Her barge, the *Zeehond*, she had told him always lay up at the Maxhaven, a dock on the other side of the river. He decided to go and see her.

He crossed the river by the Willems Bridge and in a little while had lost himself. He turned down a side street towards the river and entered a small café to ask his way.

Four seamen were playing cards at a table in one corner and the barman was scratching a label off the mirror behind the bar. He looked at Furse in the mirror and nodded.

'Cognac.'

The man served him and Furse as he paid, said :

'How do I find the Maxhaven?'

'Straight down the street. Go right, keeping behind the shipyard. Then, if you don't watch your step, you'll fall right in it. English?'

'Yes.'

'What's your boat?'

'The *Arletta*.'

'Never heard of her. What line?'

'Edward Furse Limited.'

'Never heard of it. What are you – steward?'

'No. Captain.'

The barman grinned. 'Sure. I own this bar, too. You don't have to tip me. I don't know what to do with my money as it is.' He put his big hand over the change that lay between them and slid it into his pocket. Furse felt he was a man he could get to like easily. As he turned away from the bar and sat down at a table a car drew up outside the place. A door slammed and there was the sound of the car moving away.

A man came into the bar. To his surprise Furse saw that it was Pieter. Pieter gave him a glance and then turned towards the barman.

'Coca-cola.'

Furse realized that Elsa had not sat long at her table after he had left her. Probably Rohner and Pieter had been waiting close by for her. He was a fool not to have thought of that. They had reached the point now where they hoped that violence would convince him of their intention not to be forced out of this business. If he asked for police protection it would involve him in explanations he least wanted to give.

Furse drained his glass of cognac slowly. A core of frustration was hardening inside him. At times he had been able to tell himself that, if he wished, he could withdraw from this whole affair. But, at this moment, there was no withdrawal except the ignominy, which his pride rejected at once, of going up to Pieter and asking to be taken to Rohner in order to make terms. The thought made him swear angrily to himself. This was something which had to move onwards, himself a tight-rope walker too inexpert to turn in midpassage and make his way back.

Pieter had half finished his coca-cola and stood at the counter cracking his knuckles now and again, a sound which irritated the barman and made him glance over his shoulder testily.

Furse got up and went out. There was little light in the street and a faint breeze blowing up from the river brought a warm, damp smell of mud. After a while he heard Pieter's footsteps behind him. At the bottom of the street he turned to the right and found himself in a narrow asphalt walk which ran along the back of a shipyard. On his left was a high wooden fence, on his right the long, blank-faced brick side of a factory. Half-way down the run of brick wall a bracket lamp hung out over the path giving a thin, unfriendly light. From beyond the wooden fence came the noise of riveting machines and the intermittent hiss of compressed air escaping. High overhead Furse saw the leggy steelwork of a crane, its great counter-weight poised aloft like a dead moon.

Beyond the lamp Furse stopped. He heard Pieter coming steadily along and then saw him enter the aura of light. Pieter halted. Furse went on and now he saw that at the far end of the walk a car was drawn up broadside to him. A man got out of the car and began to come towards him.

Furse watched the man moving down on him and from behind he heard the approach of Pieter. With Pieter alone he could have made some kind of showing which would, at least, have left him his pride. With the two of them he would have no chance.

He turned and found a foothold on the runner at the bottom of the fence and reached for the top. He pulled himself up quickly, his feet drumming against the wooden boards. He dropped to the other side and began to run.

The yard was a great expanse of black and grey shadows, stretching away like an enormous waste to the dim sweep of the river. From ahead of him came the bicker of a drill and away to his right rose the enormous bulk of three cargo boats high and dry at the head of the slips. They lay there like stranded monsters, their great shapes rising dark and still to the thin drift of stars. From the farthest ship came the snatch of men singing as the noise of the drill died and then the sudden peacock-blue spread of an acetylene torch, flaring like an exotic flower against the night.

There was no pride in him now, only a quick desire to find company and safety. He was a fool to have left the café, he told himself. He should have stayed there in safety . . . But there was no safety. Somewhere, sometime, Rohner would have come to him . . . He was running down the darkness of an alley, running towards nothing, just pinning his hopes on movement like a hunted animal.

He saw Pieter's companion coming across the yard from his right and knew that he was being headed off from the ship where the men were working. He swung away from him, across a waste of loose cinders, twisting between piles of old boiler plates and the fantastic curves of rusty propellers. Another burst of flame from the acetylene torch showed him a landscape stiff and dead, a cold geometrical maze of shapes through which he ran, fending himself off with his hands from their hostile edges and blades. The light died and he tripped over a length of steel rail. He fell, rolling and bunching and felt the scrape of loose cinders against the palms of his hands. He lay there, the breath driven violently from his body, and momentarily he was seized with a mad desire to abandon all action and flight. But from behind him came the thud of running footsteps . . . the sound beat into his ears, ominous and persistent. He began to pull himself up, his hands – cut and raw from the fall – reaching out and grasping cold steel, his breath returning, an angry reaching for air that now matched a growing anger in his mind.

He was up and running again, and as he went a tumult of thoughts hammered in his mind. Damn Rohner . . . Damn his own stupidity in allowing himself to be cornered like this . . . He was going on . . . Nothing was going to stop him. What he'd started he would finish.

From high in the night sky a great cone of arc light suddenly flared across the yard. Furse saw the black and silver gleam of water before him, the grey shapes of wet stones and the long length of an old iron barge tilted against the mud of a deep dock, a great gulf that cut right across his path. He swung round and saw his pursuers a hundred yards behind him, converging on him down the spokes of an invisible wheel.

For a moment he hesitated, then swung right along the dock, racing towards the great bulk of the towering hulls that lay like stranded sea monsters under the arc lights. He saw the man on his right swing across to intercept him. At first he thought he might escape him, but as he pounded along the dockside, the distance between them narrowed and he knew that they must meet. A fierce exultation began to rise in him . . . one man, one man across his path and beyond him the lights, the workmen and safety.

They met, his pursuer leaping a pile of timber to face him and Furse saw that it was not Pieter. It was a strange face, bone-white, ugly in the soft golden fall of the flickering arc light. The man leapt at him, his right hand swinging high with some black object held in it. Furse heard the whistle as the weapon struck at him, but he twisted, swung sideways, and came up under the man's arm. They crashed together and went down in a vicious swirl of arms and legs. The pale face lay below Furse and he hit out, his fist smashing against flesh. He heard a quick sob of pain from the other. He struck again, angry with a wild desire to free himself. A hand reached for his throat and held him, the nails biting into his skin. He tore himself away, struck and rolled over and then was free.

He leapt to his feet and swung away, seeing as he ran the great figure of Pieter tearing down on him from behind. The arc light died and he was running in a heavy, almost tangible darkness, forcing his way through it. In a few seconds he felt his feet strike ooze and then the hard concrete of the hauling runways that led to the nearest ship. Two acetylene flares blossomed far across the yard and, in their light, he saw the ship's side rising above him, black and sheer.

About the bulge of her keel and bilge was a bewildering pattern of blocks and scaffolding. He glanced behind him and saw that the other man had risen and was now running with Pieter. They came on deliberately, keeping together, a purposeful, menacing pair . . . the patience of two hounds who know that sooner or later they will run down the fastest quarry.

Furse went in under the bulge of the keel and a gap in the steel plating was shown up by a thin light that came from inside the ship. Distant now, the drill broke into a mad chatter. Furse reached up for the edge of the gap and got a grip on a long length of batten. He swung his feet off the ground, feeling his breath forced from him with the effort, and curled his legs upwards, reaching for the other side of the gap. He twisted over and pulled himself to his feet inside the ship. Ahead of him was a single electric bulb, hanging in a high vault of raw wooden struts and bulkheads. A ladder reached down from somewhere in the gloom above the light. Furse went up the ladder, across a darkness that smelled of fresh wood shavings and through a door in whose frame a thin stipple of stars was framed, and found himself on a lower deck. He ran forward hoping to find a way down, and behind him he heard the beat of feet striking the deck. His knees suddenly hit against the hidden side of a deck cover and he pitched forward and came to rest with a thud against a stack of steel pipes in the lee of the rail. He got up, shaken, a wave of nausea passing over him. Standing there he saw that the rest of the deck run was devoid of timbers, a great black gulf. He turned, leant over the rail and shouted towards the other ship on which the workmen were busy, shouted, hoping, too, that there might be men somewhere in the bowels of this ship who would come to his help. But his voice was lost against the chattering of the drills.

He moved away from the rail, knowing he must get to the other ship, but as he did so Pieter and the other man came out onto the deck.

He stood there, trapped, waiting for them, and with each step they took the cold fury inside him mounted until he was almost impatient for them to close with him. As though they, too, shared his impatience they suddenly flung themselves at him. He met them, his left and then his right fist moving swiftly, striking with a smooth desperation at the face of the man at Pieter's side. The man grunted and staggered backwards and, as he did so, Pieter swung in and hit Furse on the softness of skin just below the ear. The blow dazed him, but he came back at Pieter, his fist crashing into his face.

He stood there, swaying and striking, hearing the sob of his own breath, feeling the cruel shock of blows on his body while his own fists hammered at the turmoil of flesh and violence that crowded upon him. He fought now like an animal, knowing no fear, only a savage compulsion to go on battering and pounding at the faces that pressed upon him. He threw himself forward against bodies that seemed to have the hardness and dimensions of a cliff, trying to crowd the arms that hammered at him with the precision of mechanical contrivances. He drove his knee upwards and a blue gleam from the far torches showed him Pieter's face, angry, the mouth open sucking momentarily at the air. Furse slammed his fist upwards, hitting the clean line of jaw and he heard Pieter swear, a thin exclamation in Dutch. Then his own feet were kicked away from under him and, as he fell, the other man hit him on the side of the head and he went down. He forced himself to his feet, hitting out viciously. They fell back from him for a moment and then came in again. A foot crashed against his knee. He flung himself forward, mad with a desire to strike and go on striking, feeling his own body take their violence as though it were something remote and detached from him. Then, out of the confusion, a blow hit him under the ear, a blow not of flesh, but from something hard and unyielding. He went down, a red-streaked blackness gathering about him.

He tried to rise, but the air whistled violently as the blackjack struck him down again and again. He lay very still in the darkness, his breath rasping in the sudden stillness, beaten but in some odd way still stupidly conscious.

They went through his pockets and examined his wallet. He felt them turn him over and heard them talking softly, heard Pieter say in Dutch, 'He has nothing on him.'

Pieter bent down and pulled him to a sitting position. He

shook him until his eyes opened and then very carefully, like a small child sent with a message, said:

'In the morning you will come and talk to Mynheer Rohner. He will be glad to see you.'

The hand released him and he dropped back against the steel pipes. He lay there, hearing them go, and feeling that all eternity did not hold enough time to give him the sleep he craved ...

A long time afterwards, moving in a fantasy, he got up and made his way stiffly to the yard. He climbed the fence and went down the narrow walk and out to a cobbled quay side. A dozen barges lay moored together in the square basin, drifts of thin smoke coming up from their chimneys and a line or two of washing flapping in the night air. The word 'Maxhaven' on a wall swam before him, and the thought of Constanta filled his dazed mind. He began to search along the barges for the *Zeehond*. He found her tied up in the angle of the entrance jetty and the quay wall. He dropped aboard, walked the narrow deck, his fingers touching the slope of the hatch covers to help his balance, and stopped at a door in the superstructure over the stern. Above him was a glass run of windows around the wheel-house. He knocked on the door and waited.

Constanta Straatsma opened the door and in the light behind her he saw an old man and a round-faced elderly woman in an overall sitting at a table playing cards. There was a little pot of French marigolds on top of a tall terracotta stove and the radio was playing quietly.

He smiled at Constanta and said thickly, 'I was coming to see you ... Couple of thugs beat me up ...'

Constanta took his arm and brought him inside and sat him on a chair.

'Oom Paul – we have a little brandy left?'

The old man nodded and rose and she herself moved across the room, passing through a small door, and Furse heard the sound of water running. The old man came to the table with a bottle and a glass.

The brandy bit into his throat and made him cough.

Constanta came back and put a bowl of hot water on the table. Capably and gently, she began to bathe his cuts. The touch of her hands on him was comforting, tempting him almost to relax, to sink back into the bliss of abandoning himself to her care.

'You've been very kind . . .' he murmured. 'I ought not to have come here . . .'

'I'm glad you did.' She took his hand and began to wash the dirt from the abrasions on the palm. Looking down at him, she saw his eyes close slowly and his head sway, and she guessed the fatigue in him. A slow spate of tenderness moved inside her.

'You need a good night's rest. You'd better turn in here—'

He came back quickly. 'No . . . I can't let you do that. My hotel isn't far—'

She shook her head, smiling at him.

'You're not fit to go back there tonight.' Her voice was firm and determined, masking the compassion in her.

Furse saw her half turn to Oom Paul and, through a growing encroachment of sleep, he heard her say, 'He can have my bunk . . .' and Furse knew that he had no strength to argue with her.

CHAPTER SIX

When he woke it was daylight. On the boards over his bunk was a dappled movement of sunlight and he could tell that they were moving. There was a sturdy throb of a motor and the regular *slap slap* of water. He lay there for a while going over the strangeness of his surroundings with a quiet curiosity. There were four roses in a metal holder at the foot of the bunk and a little shelf of books on the far wall. A small desk was fastened to the forward bulkhead and a swinging curtain in one corner gave him a glimpse of hanging dresses and shoes on stretchers.

He sat up. His jacket was hanging beside the bunk and he had just found his cigarettes when Constanta came in without knocking. She held out a mug of coffee to him. She was wearing a skirt and blouse and her legs were bare and sunburnt.

'I thought you might be awake. I looked in an hour ago and you were dead to the world.' She was looking at him a little anxiously.

'The last thing I remember is someone called Oom Paul putting me to bed,' he said, sipping at the coffee.

'He's the skipper. You're wearing his pyjamas. Do you feel all right now?'

'Yes, thank you. A bit stiff, but otherwise . . .'

'Oom Paul went along this morning early and paid your hotel bill and brought your things. You told us you had to return to Dintelsaas today. Did we do right?'

'Of course. You've been very kind. And I've kept you out of your bunk, too.'

'There's another cabin. Why should those men attack you?'

He put the coffee down and saw that she was watching him with a curious look on her face.

He shrugged his shoulders. 'They were after my wallet, I suppose.'

'Did they get it?'

'No.'

They were silent for a moment, awkwardness hanging between them. He was tempted to tell her the truth, not only about the men and his wallet, but about himself, and the temptation was strengthened by his liking for her. He pushed the desire from him. She interested him, stirred his curiosity to know what her relationship with Sluiter had been, but he had no guarantee that she might not be equally curious about him. To tell her the truth would be rash. He was sorry about it for he would have liked his dealings with her to be quite uncomplicated. She was an attractive woman. That was all he wanted her to be.

She said suddenly, 'Who is Jimmy?'

'Did I talk about him?'

'A bit – when we were getting you in here.'

'He's my boy—'

'Oh, I see.' Unreasonably Constanta felt disappointed. It was an unexpected aspect of him. 'You're married?'

Furse shook his head. 'No. I was – but it all went on the rocks.' Then, seeing she was uncomfortable, he went on : 'We're under way, aren't we? I must get dressed and come up.'

Constanta nodded. 'We'll be in Dordrecht very soon. You can get a bus to Dintelsaas from there. We loaded up in Rotterdam yesterday evening. We don't stay long in one place. But it's a good life if you like being on the water and are content with a small profit.' It was odd, she thought, from the moment they had arrived in Rotterdam she had found herself thinking about him, hoping he would come and see her.

When he came on deck later they were running down the river to Dordrecht and already the towers and roof tops of the town were showing above a line of trees. The *Zeehond* was a diesel-engined barge, a long, low broad-beamed vessel with a raised wheel-house and living quarters aft, a capacious run of hold space and further living quarters in the bows. It was here that Constanta had her little cabin in which Furse had slept. Behind they were towing a dead-barge, laden down to the gunwales almost and with Oom Paul's wife at the tiller. Now and again Oom Paul would shout something to her from the wheel-house and she would nod for a moment and then go back to her knitting.

Constanta was sitting on the dinghy lashed to the small foredeck and she was peeling potatoes. Furse got out his knife and joined her. The river was full of shipping : great strings of barges, breasting the tide like families of solemn otters, a sailing barge with flaring sides, curved gaff and loose-footed sail, woodwork shining with varnish, and a few tramp and cargo steamers, their rusty dented bows high in ballast, their sirens lowing to clear the fairway like mildly irritated bulls moving across the crowded farmyard.

They sat there talking in the June sunlight, and the peace and contentment of the river seemed to move into both of them. The strangeness and strain between them had gone. To Constanta it seemed that he had been there many times before, chatting to her, making her laugh now and again, and all the while his big, neat hands worked quickly. It was a characteristic of his which she liked, the easy efficiency of his movements, the precise control of the big, lazy body when he was engaged in a job . . . She saw the thin glitter of sunlight on the hairs of his wrists, the brown smoothness of his forearm muscles, and she surprised a sudden impulse in herself to reach out and touch him. She was annoyed with herself at the thought but, even as she repressed the impulse, her mind had gone racing on to the reflection that it was months since any man had kissed her, or she had even wanted to be kissed, wanted to feel an arm strong and possessive around her waist.

'What are you thinking about?' Furse said. 'You're not peeling those potatoes, you're massacring them.'

'I'll never make a good housewife.' She laughed, covering her embarrassment.

'No? I'd take a chance on it any day. So would any man.'

It was said jokingly, but she wished he had meant it even while she rejected her own immaturity of thought, and told herself not to act like a schoolgirl.

The confluence of the river at Dordrecht opened up before them and the town swam up on the breast of the river, still and reflected, like something out of a canvas by Vermeer.

When the *Zeehond* berthed Furse stayed aboard and had lunch and afterwards walked into the town to catch a bus.

Constanta had told herself that she would not go with him to the bus, but in the end she went. They walked through the town side by side and Furse held her arm. It was a nice arm to hold, he thought, and without any arrogance knew that had it been dark he would have kissed her good-bye. She liked him, he knew, and he liked her. At any other time, he would have tried to improve his acquaintance with her. But he had work to do, a task ahead of him which would demand all his time and thought.

Back on the barge Constanta found Oom Paul's wife Klara knitting outside the deck-house. Klara looked up at her pensively. Then she said :

'You like him ?'

'He was in trouble. We had to help him.'

'Of course. But why today you wear a skirt and blouse instead of trousers? You think he might mistake you for a man ?'

'Klara !'

Klara laughed. 'I don't remember any other man ever gave you quite that look in your face before.'

'What look ?'

'Like a cat full of milk.'

Furse was back on the *Arletta* by six o'clock. Now that he was on his own again, the threat of trouble from Rohner became insistent. Sooner or later the man would realize that he could not be forced into working with him. When he did, sheer vindictiveness could drive him to extremes. Furse remembered Charlie's remark about bodies in the Maas, and for a moment he had an ugly picture of his own body . . .

75

floating, grotesque. He pushed the idea away from him quickly. Things weren't as bad as all that. So far, he doubted whether the man would have traced him to the *Zeehond*. For the time being he had some grace and he meant to use it. The task which lay ahead of him was to find out where in the stretch of water called the Haringvliet was located some mark which was known as the Seven Flies. The words *Zeven vliegen* written on Sluiter's overlay indicated, he felt pretty certain, a fixed mark by which the tracing could be orientated on the 192 chart. Unless he found the place he might just as well go back to England.

He went out to Dintelsaas just as it was growing dark. An hour later he was in the Haringvliet and running gently on the motor towards the occulting buoy light which marked the island of Tien Gemeten. He entered the channel known as the Vuile Gat running along the northern side of the island where there were two or three fathoms right up to the shore and dropped anchor, lying a few yards off shore. He went below, locked himself in, took his revolver from the water-tank, had a liberal whisky for nightcap and was asleep within ten minutes. But he slept on the edge of wakefulness, in a way which he had not known since he had left the Army.

The next morning as the first light was breaking he was up and busy. There were lazy little coils of vapour rising from the surface of the slack tide and among the rushes on the shore of the island reed buntings were calling harshly to one another. After making sure he was not watched, he went over the side in the dinghy and unscrewed his bow and stern name-plates, replacing them with new ones bearing the name *Felicia*. They were false plates he had carried with him ever since he had started to work with Charlie, but this was the first time he had used them. He knew that one of the ways Rohner would try to find him would be by telephoning the lock-keepers and harbour-masters in the various stretches of the Maas and asking for the *Arletta*. The new name, he hoped, would give him cover for a couple of days at least. What Rohner's next move would be was hard to say. If he could only stay free of the man for a few days and discover the whereabouts of the Seven Flies, then he could put the whole position to Charlie. He knew only too well that the business of looking for the Seven Flies, the simple process of asking questions, would eventually draw attention to himself – but, since it could not be avoided, it was a risk he had to take. His only defence against Rohner was a constant watchfulness. He had to admit to himself that it was a situation with very little comfort in it for himself. If he did not find the Seven Flies – then everything failed and he could go back to England and from there send Molenaar the whole story – but it was an unattractive prospect. Somewhere close by there was a fortune waiting to be picked up. It was going to take a great deal of force or fear to turn him away. Wherever he went, he decided, he would carry his revolver with him.

As the tide began to ebb he ran down the Vuile Gat until he was about half-way along the island of Tien Gemeten. Then he made over to the north shore of the channel and slipped into the stone-walled cut which ran up into Nieuwendijk harbour. There were only a few houses at the head of the quay and at low-water he had three feet of depth which was not enough for the *Arletta*, but he moored her with springs fore and aft to prevent her surging with the rise and fall of the tide. It was no good sailing about the river in the cutter. She was too easily recognized, despite her false name. He got the outboard motor from the stern locker and fixed it to the dinghy. While he was working a boy came down and asked him if he wanted any milk or eggs and he gave the lad a list of provisions which he promised to have aboard by the evening.

Furse asked him, 'Do you know any place around here called *Zeven vliegen*?'

The boy did not.

He decided to work the north shore from Hitsertsche Kade up to Hellevoetsluis and on the south side from Stellendam down to Den Bommel. By the afternoon he had worked the whole of the north bank up to Bakkershuisje just abreast of the seaward end of Tien Gemeten. But here, as

77

there was a strong west wind blowing which was throwing up a nasty chop across the current and making the dinghy uncomfortable, he decided to head over to the south shore to Stadschehoeck and work downstream in the lee of Overflakkee. The procedure he followed was simple, but, he felt, effective. If there was a post office, he inquired there. Then he tried the harbour or lock-master, and then if there was a café or bar open he tried there. But nowhere did he have any luck and he soon became tired of himself and his parrot-like question.

He got tired of the *put-put* of the outboard motor and nearing Den Bommel he ran out of petrol and had to row ashore, wade through a foot of mud and slime with a can and walk into the village.

At eight o'clock that night he was back at Nieuwendijk. A whole day had passed without a glimmer of hope. All day his impatience had grown. Time was a currency he could not afford to squander. He had to get results – and quickly – otherwise he would be in trouble. The boy was waiting with his provisions and he made himself a supper of fried eggs and new bread washed down with Oranjyboom beer which he had bought at Den Bommel and was asleep by ten o'clock, sleeping again on the lip of anxiety, ready to flash into action at the least alarm.

The next morning, at the turn of the tide, he was out of the harbour and racing down the Vuile Gat on the breast of the outgoing ebb and with a fine south-easterly wind pushing him along. After the dinghy work it was a pleasure to sail again.

Seven Flies . . . he kept saying to himself. He *had* to find the place, house, landmark, whatever it might be. His failure the previous day had not damped his excitement nor his optimism. He would find it. He had to find it. Kapitan Walter Maserling had used it as a mark; Maserling was a German and methodical. He would never have chosen an orienting point which might be obliterated, or so esoteric that it could only be discovered by himself. It was some permanent object whose map position could be fixed. Two hours later Furse tied up alongside the quay wall of the tramway harbour at Middelharnis on the south bank. The rest of that day he spent working up the shore, seawards, as far as Stellendam. It was a beautiful day and everything went wrong. *Zeven vliegen* meant nothing to the people he spoke to, the petrol leaked from his spare can into his food parcel, the outboard motor broke down three times with water in the carburettor and, leaning over to bring the motor inboard, his cigarettes fell into the water and it was hours before he could buy new ones. He could feel himself growing irritable and nervous under the strain of the search. He suspected every boat that passed him, hesitated outside every café and post office, obsessed by the danger that time was running out, that at any moment Rohner or one of his men would catch up with him and his search would become impossible.

When he got back to the *Arletta* very late he found that during the day some boat had come alongside awkwardly and laid a fine score two feet long in the paint of her bows. He rubbed the mark down, cursing to himself, repainted it and went below too tired to bother about supper. He lay on his bunk and drank half a bottle of whisky and finally slept heavily, fully dressed, until ten o'clock the next morning. He woke up angry at his own dejection and half convinced that he would never find the *Zeven vliegen* and that, anyway, the whole project was degenerating into a fantastic purgatory which he had devised for himself, a bumping, *put-putting* discomfort in which he motored apprehensively through eternity on the breast of the muddy Maas, with the slow-revolving arms of windmills waving sadly to him from the green polders and the patient figures of nursery-cut Friesian cows turning their gentle heads at him as he went by, their eyes full of liquid mournfulness. He thought of the array of solemn-faced Dutchmen who had stared at him after the question had been put to them, shaking their heads and somehow implying that it was a stupid question in the first place and that a man ought to have better occupation than to be going around with such a frivolous inquiry.

He had now only the strip of shore between Hellevoetsluis and Bakkershuisje to cover. He was not looking forward to going over to the small port of Hellevoetsluis. It was an obvious place for Rohner to have stationed a man. He would have to take the *Arletta* over, too. The weather looked as though it were going to change for the worse and he did not want to have to make a stormy crossing back to Middelharnis that night in the flimsy dinghy. Anyway, if he didn't strike lucky today there was nothing else he could do. He could sense his reluctance to go over growing. He was sticking his neck out . . . But he had to do it. He cursed Rohner softly as he prepared to go. Just before he was ready to leave Middelharnis a Dutchman in a blue shirt and white shorts whose steel-hulled cutter lay a little farther up the quay from him came aboard and presented him with a bottle of Schiedam gin and his apologies for having marked his boat when he had come in the previous evening. He offered to pay for the damages.

'Mynheer, I know how you must feel. I am so sorry. But just at the last moment a puff of wind caught us and my wife at the tiller was not quick enough.'

Furse told him not to worry and convinced him that he was forgiven by opening the bottle and drinking a glass with him. In the course of their talk he asked him his question, and got a familiar reply.

'There's a restaurant called the Five Flies in Amsterdam. I've never heard of a *Seven Flies* in the Haringvliet. Is it a house or a restaurant?'

'I don't know. To me it's just a name. It might even be a sand bank or a clump of trees.'

'Well, I wish I could help you. You have been very good about the damage to your boat. Five Flies – yes, Seven – no.' He was silent for a moment, his face solemn with thought. Then he said ponderously, 'Vliegen, you know, is a Dutch name. That is how the restaurant in Amsterdam is called – not after flies, but after the name of the family who started it in the sixteenth or seventeenth century. Maybe you should inquire for a family called Vliegen?'

It was an idea which had not occurred to Furse and as he sailed over to Hellevoetsluis he thought about it. He came through the harbour entrance and idled up to the landing-stage below the lock entrance. As he came alongside he went astern and called to a man standing on the quay. He flung his stern warp, saw it safely into the man's hands and then slipped forward and jumped ashore with the bow rope. He fastened it round a mooring post and then went back to the man who had helped him. He was looping the rope in a clumsy hitch round a stone bollard and, as he straightened up, Furse saw that it was Anselm Dekker. For a moment they looked at one another and then Dekker smiled. It was a smile of curious quality, half friendliness, half regret. He stood there, his blue suit rather dusty and his trousers clamped at his ankles with bicycle clips. Propped on the quay behind him was a bicycle with a tiny auxiliary motor over the back wheel.

Furse sat down on the bollard and lit a cigarette. For a while the two men looked at one another. This was the end, Furse thought. It had to happen – and here it was. A slow mood of savage depression settled over him. He had tried, and he had failed. Rohner was up with him, and this time he would not let go . . . He cursed himself for risking the run over to Hellevoetsluis. Now, he could kiss a nice little fortune goodbye. The only virtue left to him was to accept his bad luck with good grace. He glanced up at Dekker and said, 'You weren't long finding me.'

'I should have been quicker, mynheer, only I did not expect that you would do anything illegal.' Dekker nodded to the *Felicia* name-plate on the stern. 'A ship must carry the same name as her papers.'

'Where's Rohner?'

'In Rotterdam.'

'And how do you come to be here?'

'In another half-hour I was to take the ferry across to Middelharnis. I wanted to examine an English yacht, Danish pilot cutter type with one Englishman aboard, name

– *Felicia*. It has the same number of letters as *Arletta*. A pretty name, too.'

'After an aunt of mine. How long have I got before Rohner is on my tail?' His voice sounded casual, but already he knew that the last thing he could abandon was hope.

'As long as it takes me to telephone him and for him to get here. He should be here by this evening.'

He knew what was happening. It was no good accepting bad luck. Fight it, he told himself . . . there's always a chance so long as one hammers away at hope. 'If you had gone across to Middelharnis, and missed me and then found I was here this evening, he couldn't have done much until tomorrow morning,' he suggested.

'That's true, mynheer.'

'Would you like a ride on the ferry?'

Dekker smiled. He was a man of understanding. 'How much would you be prepared to pay?'

'Ten guilders.'

Dekker, shaking his head, pulled out a cigarette packet that was empty and tossed it into the water. Furse handed him a cigarette.

'Fifteen guilders, then. That's the limit. I'm not a rich man.'

'But you have hopes.'

'Why do you say that?'

'It is a hope all men retain until the last. I think I would like to go to Middelharnis.'

Furse went below and got his money. He also brought up a couple of bottles of beer and some bread and cheese which he shared with Dekker on deck. As they were eating, the ferry-boat pulled out of the tramway harbour. Dekker saw Furse's look and shrugged his shoulders.

'There is another in a couple of hours. You like our cheese?' he asked, cutting himself a thick wedge. 'Then you should go to Gouda. It is famous for its cheese. The whole town smells of it.'

'How strong is your loyalty to Rohner?'

'Thirty guilders a day and the bonus when the job is done.'

'How much is the bonus?'

'It has not been fixed yet, mynheer.'

'Do you know what all this is about?'

'Only what I guess, mynheer. There is money in it, obviously. Enough to justify either you or Rohner having killed a man called Sluiter. Would you like some advice, mynheer?'

'Why not?'

'You should go back to England. This is a pleasant country if you do not mind flatness, but there is too much water and in some places too much loneliness. A man can disappear and never be found. In the Hollandsche Diep, for instance, you can bury something in the sands of one of the *slikken* and in a couple of tides it is eight feet under and in a couple of days it is gone for ever. During the war a great many Germans disappeared like that.'

'I'll think about it.'

'I doubt it, mynheer. I shall now ride round to the ferry and have a sleep in the waiting-room. Thank you for the lunch. I do not hope to see you again, but I am afraid I shall.'

Furse watched him push his bicycle along the quay. He moved with that slow, dispirited yet persisting manner which in certain men acquires a humble dignity. It was odd, he thought, how roguery sat pleasantly on some men. There was evil in them but you could not bring yourself to believe that it was important. Charlie had it, and this man Dekker.

The moment he saw the ferry-boat go out, he went quickly ashore. For the moment he had gained a respite . . . there was still a little time left to him.

He went up to the small post office in the town. The place was empty except for a pale-faced man with a large Adam's apple behind the small serving window. Sunlight broke into a hundred jets of colour off the tiles which lined the floors and walls and there was a somnolence about the place made heavier by the frantic buzz of a fat fly trapped against one of the windows.

'Is there anyone called Vliegen who lives in the district?'

'No.' The man was sorting postcards and hardly looked at him.

'Or any place or house called the Seven Flies?'

'No.'

Something about the man's manner irritated him. He had the irrational feeling that other people, even without being told, should instinctively share his urgency to find an answer to his riddle.

'You're certain?' he asked sharply.

'Yes.' The man seemed not to have noticed the asperity in Furse's voice. He reached back and put a pile of cards in a pigeon-hole and then, as Furse turned away to the door, added, 'I've lived in this district forty years, except for three when I was in Sumatra – climate was bad for me out there so I had to come back, which was a pity because it was a good job, better than this – and my family have been living here for over two hundred years. Never met a Vliegen about here in my life. Never handled a letter for a Vliegen or a letter addressed to any Seven Flies. What are you? Police or debt collecting?'

'Neither. I'm looking for a friend.'

'If he's a sailor or a merchant seaman ask at the café down the road. Someone might know him. But he isn't a resident.'

Furse went down the road to the café. There was an old man sitting on a stone post by the door and inside four men playing cards and drinking cups of *slagroom* laced with brandy.

Furse ordered a glass of beer from a woman who came out from the back of the café. When it came he put his question to her and the four men. None of them could help him. Two of them were labourers who were working on the lock and had had a foreman of that name in Haarlem years before, and the other two suggested that he might have the name wrong. There was a farmer called Reigen higher up the Vorne Canal. The proprietress stood between them, her upper lip glistening with sweat from the heat of her kitchen, and shook her head sympathetically.

Furse gave up and leaned back. They left him alone with his beer. The heat of the afternoon had worked into him and he felt lazy and dispirited. He had been too optimistic, too excited at the prospect of easy wealth, to realize just how difficult this stage was likely to be. Perhaps, he thought, it was just as well that he was going to be unlucky. In a way it would be saving himself from himself. Bad luck might serve him better than good. It was a consolation he could not accept with any grace. He wanted the money and to hell with his conscience, wanted it more with each step that he took, wanted it particularly now that he had been beaten up by Rohner's men. In a way that savagery gave him a claim to it . . . He drained his beer and stood up. There were a few more places he could try. He had not been over to Tien Gemeten yet and anyway he could not stay in Hellevoetsluis that evening.

As he stood outside the door, the hot sunlight striking down at him, the old man sitting on the stone post rose and gave him a gentle nod. He was a very old man, his face cut and furrowed with age and his mouth sunk back into a dry, taut pucker on his shrunken gums. He was short and gnome-like, an effect heightened by a black woollen cap and a tight-fitting suit of wrinkled corduroy. He wore little gold earrings and a red jersey.

In a reedy voice, he said in good English, 'Heard what you said, though your Dutch ain't so good as you think. English, ain't you?'

'Yes.'

The old man fell into step alongside Furse who slowed his pace to accommodate him.

'Know Gravesend?'

'I've been there. Is that where you learnt your English?'

'Yes. Built boats there for fifteen years. Thames barges, before you was born. Married my wife there, before you was born. Come back here to live on charity. Me nephew. Bed and board, ounce of tobacco a week and a few guilders for drink. Good boy, but mean.'

Furse smiled and slipped him five guilders. 'Have a drink with me some time.'

The old man took it as naturally as a hen picks up corn and gave a dry chuckle. 'Looking for a friend of yours, eh? Vliegen?'

Furse gave the man a sharp look. He was old, but there was nothing wrong with his hearing or his wits, and he had the impression that the man was enjoying some joke.

'Yes. Do you know him?'

The old man nodded. 'Bet your life. See him every day when I visit my wife. She don't live with me. Like to see him?'

Furse said quickly, hope rising in him, 'You take me to Vliegen and I'll make it twenty guilders.'

'Sure?' The old man sounded a bit worried now. 'No matter what?'

'Take me to Vliegen and the money is yours.'

'This way. But not too fast, eh? Legs are going. Yes, it's a good place Gravesend, but not what it was they tell me. Time was when I seed the Thames crowded with them barges, big red sails flapping like a lot of flamingos and only a man and a boy aboard . . . Now it's all this petrol and oil stink and there ain't a river in Europe that don't smell like a sewer.'

They went slowly through the town and down a dusty side road lined with neat little market garden plots with lettuces and cabbages set out in military lines, and then past a low, white-fronted house with curving gables which held Furse's attention for a while. If the old man does put me on to it, he thought, I'll make it South Africa and we'll have a house in Dutch colonial style. He would design it himself. Maybe Jimmy would take a turn that way . . . already he had that kind of imagination and a sense of design. Momentarily he surprised in himself a nostalgia for the feeling of a good pencil and a drawing-board, a shaded lamp and the black and silver of rulers across white paper. Then it was gone as the old man paused, spat in the dust and nodded towards a low white gate.

'In there.'

They walked up a neat gravel path and on either side were trim squares of grass and smooth mounds backed by headstones.

'That's my wife,' said the old man, and he jerked his head towards a fairly new headstone at the left of the path. 'And that—' he led Furse over the grass to an angle of the surrounding wall—'is "Vliegen".'

Furse found himself looking at an old headstone in slate, worn and beautifully patinated by time. Across the top was a fine eighteenth-century carving of an angel's head, flanked by skull and cross-bones. Underneath in a delicate lettering which he knew must have been done by a true craftsman was an inscription commemorating one Johannus Vliegen of Krabbensplaat who had died in 1799.

'That's Vliegen,' said the old man a little nervously. 'The only one around here. Remember, you said twenty guilders – no matter what.'

CHAPTER SEVEN

It was not until Furse was back in the *Arletta* that it occurred to him that the old man might after all have earned his twenty guilders. Johannus Vliegen had lived on Krabbensplaat, which Furse knew was a small island off the end of Tien Gemeten. It had been a long time ago, but there might be some family association or mark on the island still which would explain the phrase 'Seven Flies'.

He looked up the island in a yachting guide, and read :—

Channels above *Hellevoetsluis* : about five miles above Hellevoetsluis an island named Krabbensplaat marks the division of the river into two channels. Shoal water extends from the upper end of Krabbensplaat to the lower end of the island of Tien Gemeten. The main buoyed fairway is through the Vuile Gat on the north side of Krabbensplaat and Tien Gemeten, while Haringvliet, no longer the principal fairway, continues along the Overflakkee shore south of the two islands. Krabbensplaat was enlarged by reclamation in 1810 and is now a small island of about 200 acres chiefly remarkable for its fine pastures.

He decided to have a look at Krabbensplatt. With Rohner soon to be on his tail he could not stop in Hellevoetsluis.

He passed the ferry-boat just outside the harbour entrance and saw Dekker standing on deck. He went upstream towards Krabbensplaat and Tien Gemeten. He had passed the little island before, hanging like a pendant off the end of Tien Gemeten, but had paid it little interest for he had imagined it to be uninhabited. He ran down the Vuile Gat, watching the island through his glasses. Its seaward end was open pasture, the banks rush-fringed, and off shore there were little patches of sand bank, rimmed with wind-blown sea-scud and now disappearing as the tide rose. Towards

Tien Gemeten the island became wooded on its banks, tall poplars with a backing of willows that hid the meadows behind. The chart showed too little water for him to risk crossing between the two islands, so he went about and ran up to the north-eastern end of the island and over into the Haringvliet.

Coming down the Haringvliet he passed open pasture, dotted here and there with willows and cut with small ditches. Nearing Tien Gemeten there was a long frontage of poplars and behind them other trees. But almost at the end of the island he noticed a break in the bank and, for a moment, as he idled by on the motor he saw a finger of water running into the island. He looked on his chart for the cut, but it was unmarked.

He stood across towards Stadschehoeck on the Overflakkee shore and anchored in three fathoms of water fifty yards from the shore and well out of the main channel. *Arletta* pointed her nose seaward to the incoming tide. Krabbensplaat was half a mile away from him and slightly forward of his starboard bow. He drew up the dinghy which he had been towing, shipped the outboard motor and went across in the early evening light. He edged in close to the south-western bank of the island. The tide was running slack close inshore. Once or twice, keeping too close alongside the bank, he grounded on sand but came off easily. He knew from his chart that the sand extended only a few yards off the shore.

When he was abreast of the mouth of the cut he shut off the motor, and decided to use an oar and scull himself in. He came in sounding now and again with his lead. There was plenty of water except over the bar at the mouth of the cut where it shallowed to just under a fathom.

The cut, about twelve feet wide at its mouth, ran up between trees, gradually widening until it was thirty feet across. Furse worked up it gently. There was no current here and the dribble of water behind the dinghy made a low, pleasant sound in the shadow of the trees. A line of ducks swung out from under the overhanging bushes to his left and kept him

company for a few yards, talking and quacking to themselves, resenting his intrusion.

Suddenly the trees dropped away and the cut opened out
into a basin lined on its left with a rough timber quay and
shoaling away elsewhere to low grass banks. The bank ahead
of him was broken by a small brick archway, covered with an
iron grille, through which the waters of a ditch were fed into
the basin. There was a motor boat tied up alongside the
quay. Furse went alongside and climbed on to the timbers.

Beyond the basin and approached by a gravel path was a
house. Until now it had been masked by the trees that lined
the lower end of the island. It sat there, flanked by poplars,
its red brick flushed to a warm glow by the setting sun. The
front was broken by three gables, their lines standing out in
graceful arabesques against the pale green of the eastern sky.
The upper windows were tall and mullioned and made gay
with folded-back shutters painted white and blue in an
intricate lozenge pattern, while the lower windows were
close-framed with ironwork that swept upwards, curved
and arrogant with the line of a swan's neck. There was a
courtyard in front of it, surrounded by a brick wall that
merged on the left with a run of stables and other outbuild-
ings.

As an architect Furse recognized it at once as a house
which had lived in the mind's eye of an artist long before it
ever went on the drawing-board. It had the dignity and presence of so much Dutch renaissance building, and then some
other quality – the beauty which only men in love with their
materials can create.

Furse walked slowly along the gravel path. In this house
had lived and died Johannus Vliegen – who had already cost
him twenty guilders, he thought wryly. But had Vliegen or
this house anything to do with a German naval captain who
had written the words *Zeven vliegen* on a map overlay? He
did not know, and at this moment he was almost convinced
that he was on a wild goose chase . . . there was this problem, then Rohner, then Molenaar probably keeping a quiet
eye on him, and other difficulties to come . . . You're crazy,

he thought, ever to have started a thing like this . . . A quarter of a million. It was a dream, and it was time he woke up.

He had his hand on the wrought-iron gateway that led into the yard and was about to push it open when he stopped. His mouth went suddenly dry, and he felt the quick excitement of his heart beating, and at the same time he was saying angrily to himself, 'You might have missed it. You blundering fool! You'd have pushed it open and gone through. You might never have seen it, never have seen the thing a German captain saw and remembered so vividly that he used it to mark a quarter of a million—'

He was staring at the gateway. Its fine iron tracery was worked with whorls and volutes of flowers. Scattered amongst the flowers, stiff and archaic in outline, were seven enormous flies. Excitement rose swiftly in him. This was it.

He lit a cigarette and his hand was steady, though he knew that inwardly there was a fine tremor in him, the tenseness delayed until this moment of realizing just what lay within his grasp.

A man came out of the house and walked across the yard towards him. He was in his shirt sleeves, wearing a dark leather waistcoat which looked as though it never left him, its creases rubbed shiny and bare like the hide of an animal. The yellow clogs on his feet made a clatter on the ground. He came right up to the gate and stared at Furse through the tracery.

'You want something, mynheer?'

The voice was soft, a little hesitant, as if he feared that even in a simple phrase there was always the danger of giving offence.

'I was just looking round. I hope you don't mind. I wondered, too, if you might have some eggs to sell? My boat's anchored across the river.'

They spoke in Dutch.

'Only duck eggs.' A hand reached out and the gate swung open. It moved gently on well-oiled rests.

'They'll do.' Furse gave him a smile as he stepped in.

'In the dairy. You are English?'

91

He had a large, tired face. The eyes were grey and friendly and, although he must have been over sixty, there was a liveliness in them which made Furse forget the deep furrows the years had put on his face. He walked firmly, but the shoulders were drawn over, making him shorter than he really was.

'Yes. English. You own the house and farm?'

'Yes. It is all mine.' There was a touch of pride in his voice, and moving with him to the dairy in one corner of the yard Furse could understand the pride. Nothing was out of place. Everything shone or was in spotless order, the paintwork, the brick pointing, the neat little flower beds, the midden within its concrete retaining walls . . . the look of the near pastures, the yard and the various implements all had a tidiness and a formal, yet elegant, arrangement that somehow made the place seem more like an illustration from a book.

As they went into the dairy, Furse commented on the neatness of the farm. The man chuckled.

'In Holland that is not unusual. And anyway Nature is such an untidy creature that a good farmer must learn to keep her in order if he wants to live happily with her.'

'She's broken quite a few farmers' hearts.'

'Ja – but not mine. You keep on at her with patience and in the end she gives in. Also you must not expect miracles. She has only a few and she goes on working them. But not new ones. Good milk from bad pasture she cannot give, nor big apples off old trees. You taste that—' He dipped a measure of milk from one of the cans and handed it to Furse. 'In the whole of Holland you won't find milk with a better cream content. I win prizes for it.' The pride was back in his voice, but there was no note of arrogance. 'In a moment I'll show you my Friesians. You have children?'

'One boy.'

'My wife and I are unlucky. But my Friesians – they are my children.'

A little later he led Furse to a home pasture at the back of the house. The light was going quickly and there was a slow mist coming up off the grass. The black and white cattle stood patiently in the hock-deep grass, immobile now, given over to the trance of deep thought so that each one seemed carved and enamelled by some meticulous hand. A trio of bats cut and winged their way through the purpling air above them.

Jan Beukleman – he had given his name to Furse as they talked – whistled gently and the immobility of the herd was broken by a slow movement of heads.

'Each one I know,' he said. 'Each one from a calf I have seen grow. You must meet Kadza. She has children in many parts of the world . . . Africa, South America, all over. Kadza! Kadza!' he called.

One of the cows turned and came slowly across the pasture, leaving great swathes of dew marks on the grass, the bell at her throat marking the sway of her forequarters with a hollow, musical note. She came up to them, thrust her soft muzzle at Beukleman and blew a great gust of sweet, warm breath as though she sighed, ecstatically, at the touch of Beukleman's hands on her head.

As they turned away and walked back to the little quayside, Furse asked : 'Do you and your wife run this farm without help?'

Beukleman nodded. 'Yes.'

'How did you get on during the war?' Furse asked casually.

Beukleman was silent for a while. Then he said, 'It was hard. In the early days most of my cattle were taken. I saw a lifetime's work go – like that.' He snapped his fingers. 'But later it was better. We were left alone. Towards the end, you know, these waters—' he jerked his head towards the Haringvliet, '—were dangerous. Our partisans used to wait for any German boats that came along. But it was not something I could do. War is evil from whichever side you see it, and all soldiers are men. In the house back there we helped everyone who came to us in trouble, our own partisans, British commandos, Belgians and once or twice even Germans who needed help. You think that is wrong?'

'No, I don't think I do.'

'You were a soldier, then?'

Furse nodded. For a moment he wanted to ask if Jan Beukleman had ever helped a German naval captain called Walter Maserling. Then he decided against it, not because he thought Beukleman would deny it, but in order to avoid having to explain his question. The old man thought he had come to the island out of simple curiosity. He wanted to leave things like that. There was something about Jan Beukleman which, in the short time he had been with him, had affected him deeply. There was a sincerity and honesty about the man and his love for his farm and his beasts which made Furse strangely dissatisfied with himself and yet, at the same time, glad that he had met him.

Jan Beukleman walked with him across the courtyard as far as the gate. Furse had the impression that the man was lonely and welcomed company. As Beukleman held the gate open for him, Furse nodded at the design.

'It's a nice piece of work – but why the design of the seven flies?'

Beukleman smiled. 'When the house was built – that was in the early eighteenth century – it was for a family called Vliegen. There were seven of them, all brothers, and I suppose the gate was just a fanciful idea. In the end only one brother lived here. But since his time the house has changed hands two or three times.'

It was almost dark when Furse reached the *Arletta*. All the way across the river the outboard engine had seemed to beat a fixed refrain in his mind. *I've got it. I've got it.* With Beukleman he had been forced to curb his excitement and hope. But now, he could give rein to his feelings. From what he remembered of the overlay it seemed a fair supposition that the stones would be in the river somewhere. From the letters he had destroyed from Sluiter's file he knew that Maserling had come up this river in a launch and that the launch had been sunk – but whether the stones had remained aboard or Maserling had cached them somewhere had not been stated. Recalling the little dotted circle and

94

then the cross which marked the Seven Flies he felt sure that whichever way the overlay might be oriented the ring of dots would strike the river somewhere. A sunken launch. It couldn't be in much more than a couple of fathoms near the island . . . one could dive without any elaborate outfit . . . a steel deed-box, small enough to lift. It sounded too easy . . . Perhaps it was. Anyway, his job now was to get on to Charlie. Between them they could fix the whole thing up.

Before he had supper he went over the side in the dinghy and put *Arletta*'s true name-plates back. He worked happily, whistling to himself. There was no doubt in him now. He was too near success to cloud this moment with anxiety about Rohner. Charlie would help him to deal with Rohner. It was comforting to think of Charlie who knew all the answers and was ready for any difficulty. The Nieuwe Hollandse Bank had been covered with insurance and reparations by the Allies out of recovered loot from Germany. They might still be a little out of pocket – but any bank could stand that. Nobody was really going to lose anything, and he . . . Well, you never got anywhere unless you looked after yourself.

His elation stayed with him, a sustaining extravagance of spirit which coloured his thoughts. He sat on deck, smoking and watching the stars sway gently in reflection on the face of the waters while he carefully planned how he should lay out his wealth when it came.

It was drizzling with rain the next morning and the water was cold about his feet as he swabbed down the decks. Through the moving folds of rain he could catch a glimpse of Krabbensplaat now and again. The great poplars swayed in the wind, their dark crests tossing as though they were the plumes of horses in some solemn cortège. The wind was in the west and promised more rain. Long, restless, coffee-coloured rollers capped the run of the tide and the *Arletta*, feeling the stir of water under her, danced and swung awkwardly as if she were anxious to be away from her anchorage.

He went below to make himself breakfast before moving

off and, as he stood by the galley, he heard the sound of a motor come beating across the water, the note growing louder each moment. He put his head out of the hatchway and saw that a white motor launch was bearing down on the *Arletta*. It came across the tide clumsily, shaking its stubby bows and sending up a white splatter of foam. It was a type of craft for which Furse had no affection, a floating gin palace with a run of glass and chromium cabin-top, over-powered, and a death trap if anyone were unwise enough to take it outside the river in anything like a sea. As it came nearer he saw that it was called the *Yssel*. He saw, too, that standing forward of the cabin trunk, a yellow oilskin wrapped loosely round him, was Rohner.

He swore to himself. He had hoped to get away from Krabbensplaat before Rohner caught him up. Dekker must have worked quickly. He dropped his hand into his jacket pocket and felt the bulk of his Luger. If Rohner was bringing trouble he was also going to be met with it.

The launch crossed across his bows and then came slowly abreast, hanging a few yards away from him, the motor throttled down. At the wheel was Pieter, also in oilskins. There was no sign of anyone else. The launch hung there, holding its place and, as Furse watched the two men, part of his mind was telling him that Pieter was no fool at handling a boat. Nothing was said for a while. Rohner, his head bare, the gold-flecked hair tousled boyishly, raised a hand in greeting and then said something over his shoulder to Pieter. The turn of his head brought the rain-polished face into profile.

The launch edged in until it was a yard from the *Arletta*'s rail. Furse went forward, a fender in one hand and the Luger in the other.

He said evenly, 'If you try and come aboard, I'll use this – and think of some story for the police afterwards.'

'I want to talk to you,' called Rohner. 'You won't need that. Let me come aboard.'

Furse shook his head. 'You stay where you are. There's nothing you can say to me—'

96

'Please—' For a moment Rohner was conciliatory. 'You've a right to be angry. I apologize for the way I treated you. I made a mistake about you. Let me come aboard.'

Furse hesitated between telling the man to go to hell and letting him come aboard.

'All right,' he said brusquely. 'But don't try anything funny.'

Pieter brought the launch in. For a while the two boats rose and pitched and then, choosing his moment, Rohner jumped aboard the *Arletta*. The *Yssel* at once swung away and went upstream.

Furse, his revolver held ready, backed Rohner to the stern.

'Open your oilskin,' he said and, when Rohner did so, he ran his hand over the man's clothes. Rohner was unarmed.

'I never carry them – except in a real emergency,' said Rohner pleasantly.

They went below and Furse faced Rohner across the saloon table. His revolver was on the bunk cushion beside him.

Rohner looked around, genuinely interested, and then said : 'This is a nice boat. Not like that tub I've hired. You could go anywhere in this.'

'Come to the point.'

'I will. For a moment I imagined we might overcome our antipathy. But, anyway, we've something stronger than friendship to hold us together.'

'Which is?'

'A quarter of a million pounds,' Rohner was looking straight at him now. 'You're ahead of me so far, Mr Furse, but you can't shake me off. I can wait. You're looking for something up here – something which will put you on to the real thing. Elsa at least learned that from Sluiter. I don't think you've found what you're looking for yet. But you will. When you do – I'm going to be standing by. When you get your hands on a quarter of a million, I shall be there – and then we'll talk about a partnership.'

'You're going too fast, Rohner. At this moment I'm not

even sure I won't go to the police and give them the whole story. That would put you and Elsa in a bad position.'

Furse saw the polite smile go from Rohner's face, leaving it cold and predatory. His voice when he spoke was harsh and threatening.

'Go to the police and both of us will swear that you were working with us and knew all about it. I've got your signature from the hotel you stayed at in Rotterdam. I can fix up letters from you to me. Molenaar is no fool but his weakness is always being too suspicious. He'll know that you came to see me in Rotterdam, that I've come down the Vorne Canal this morning to see you, that wherever you are there I am. He'll think we're working together. Keep that in your mind, Mr Furse. Inform on us . . . and you pull yourself in as well.'

His words came clear and hard above the noise of the creak and strain of the *Arletta* as she rose and fell, and behind them Furse caught the intense, bitter note of a man who knows no scruples.

'I'm a good listener,' said Furse, 'but I've had enough. You can do what you damned well like, but you don't scare me, and you're not putting me off.'

Rohner stood up, buttoning his oilskin about him, wet drops shaking from it to the table top. 'Make a deal with me, and I'll stick to it.'

Furse smiled. 'You're wasting your time. Now get off my boat!'

Rohner shrugged his shoulders, and went up on deck. Furse followed him. They stood there, the rain beating into their faces while the launch came up towards them.

Before he went over the side Rohner turned to Furse.

'Think it over,' he said, his voice heavy with dislike. 'I shall be around. I shan't interfere until the last moment. Then I shall come in. It's up to you what kind of deal we make then . . . a friendly one, or—' he nodded towards the revolver which Furse held.

When Rohner had gone, Furse went below and had his breakfast. He shut all speculation from him. The first thing he had to do was to get in touch with Charlie and – with

Rohner about – it was better to do that as far away from this spot as possible. He decided that he would run down to Dordrecht and telephone Charlie from there.

In half an hour he was under way, running down the Overflakkee shore with the west wind strong on his beam.

It took him three hours to make Dordrecht where he ran into the yacht haven just above the bridge and tied up at the staging by the clubhouse.

He went ashore and telephoned Charlie, but a woman's voice answered him and told him that Charlie was away in Amsterdam. After a little hesitation she gave him a telephone number and he eventually got Charlie on the telephone in Amsterdam.

He found that Charlie would not be free of his business in Amsterdam until the next day, and arranged with him that they would meet on the *Arletta* at six o'clock the following evening.

'I come right through from Amsterdam by road, sir. No point in you coming up to Rotterdam. I call in at my flat and pick up some things? Or perhaps you like that I don't do that?'

'Yes, Charlie – you pick up your things on the way through.'

'Good. Everything go all right with you?'

'Yes. So far ...'

'Take a tip, major. You sleep in a hotel tonight. That boat of yours is draughty. I don't want you should catch any colds what turn to rigor mortis. And lock the door.'

'I'm sleeping on the boat. I can lock the door there – and have something behind it.'

'OK, colonel.'

'You've promoted me.'

'I think from sound of your voice you deserve it. By the way – your friend Molenaar had tea with me the other day.'

'I've seen nothing of him since Middelburg.'

'You will soon is my bet.'

In Rotterdam, Herman Molenaar was talking to the chief

of his department. His chief was a thin, vigorous man with sunken cheeks, a bald head and a shrewd eye for mistakes and uncertainties. He leaned forward across his desk and now and then tapped the sails of the little silver windmill model which formed part of his inkwell. It was a movement which made Molenaar nervous and took his mind off what he was saying so that his words became hurried and stilted as though he were reading evidence in a court.

'I've had a good man on him. Occasionally he's lost him for a while, but that always happens. Then there's the report from England. All the rest I've handled myself.' He paused wondering what his chief's reaction would be.

The man spun the windmill and said, 'I wish this rain would stop. It spoils my petunias.' Then he leaned back and raised his left hand, staring at the palm as though he could read something there. 'The Bank are getting anxious . . .' His voice had a gentle, humorous quality but was produced with a studied resonance as though he were proud of its range. 'Yes, they're getting positively fierce about their precious stones, but we mustn't let that worry us, or hurry us, Molenaar. Anxiety is natural to a bank and worry is anathema to a policeman.'

'Yes, sir.' Molenaar was not sure whether he was agreeing with him or missing some possible irony.

'As far as Sluiter is concerned, I wouldn't say you've got much that helps. There was a woman staying with him in his London hotel, probably Dutch. But she didn't travel over with him. And you can't trace her. He didn't have a mistress or a wife, or if he did he kept them out of sight. You've got nothing really, have you?'

'No, sir.'

'Never mind – that's how it often is right up to a few hours before an arrest. Let's see what you have about Furse. The English Customs people suspect he's done some smuggling, but they can't prove it. Over here we know he knows and has had contact with our friend Ponz and our elegant Mr Rohner – between them they might be working on anything in the criminal calendar. But we mustn't forget, Molenaar, that quite a lot of innocent people have odd friends. We know that Furse has been sailing in the Haringvliet area and that he even changed the name of his boat for a while . . . Odd that, but not criminal.' He made a long humming note in his throat and then went on, 'I wonder . . . Interesting, isn't he? However, at the moment you've got nothing against him, either for murder or for the other thing. He might know nothing at all about the Bank's stones. That's the trouble. He could go on giving that impression right up to the moment when he grabbed them from wherever they are. That would be a bit late perhaps for us to do anything. If it happened the Bank's anxiety would become frenzy and there might be departmental changes around here. What do you suggest, Molenaar?'

Molenaar was silent. The only real suggestion he had he was afraid to offer, that was to wait and see, let time work for them. He said slowly, drawing out his words as though he might suddenly discover some hidden significance in them and save himself, 'I want a chance to go over his boat thoroughly. We might find something there . . . something to work on.'

His chief stood up and went to the window. 'It's something you might have done earlier.' Then after a pause he went on, 'Do you know the Chinese attitude towards doctors, Molenaar?'

'No, sir.'

'They pay them to keep them in good health. I think we must become Chinese doctors to the Bank and possibly to Mr Furse. Do you remember our French friend, Delacroix?'

'I won't forget him in a hurry, sir.'

'No, I suppose not. Anyhow, we'll give Mr Furse a little longer and then, if nothing comes up, we'll give him the Delacroix treatment.'

'I understand, sir.'

In Dordrecht Constanta was just leaving a marine engineering works where she had been arranging for the overhaul of her second barge. It was going to cost more than she could reasonably afford, and the barge would be out of commission for a week which meant the loss of more money. Slowly over the years since her father had died, the fight had been going against her. The end would come unless she could find fresh capital. Maybe she would finish by taking the advice of her friends – sell up and find herself a job.

On her way back she crossed the swing-bridge over the mouth of the yacht haven and saw the *Arletta* tied up by the boat-house. Furse, who was on deck, saw her and gave her a hail.

'How's the head?' she called.

'Fine. Come aboard and have a drink.'

Constanta shook her head. 'Sorry, not now. Why don't you come and have supper with us on the *Zeehond* tonight if you're free?'

Furse accepted the invitation gladly.

Constanta went back to the *Zeehond*, a suppressed excitement working in her. Every time she caught herself thinking about this man it heightened her emotions . . .

She gave Oom Paul instructions to have the other barge sent up to the yard in the morning, and then went to her cabin. She stripped off her working clothes and took a bath. One day, she thought, I'll have a bath where I can stretch my legs.

She dressed slowly, watching herself in the tall strip of glass fastened to the back of the cabin door. The rain had gone and there was yellow evening sunlight reflected through the porthole from the water outside. She slipped on a yellow dress, knowing the look Klara would give her. It was a colour which, contrasting with her dark hair and brown skin, gave her a richness, not only of looks, but of feeling. She made her face up, knowing why she was doing it, enjoying a sense of rebellion. Thick, soft red lips. Her nose . . . she could do nothing about that. It flattened a little too much at the end and turned slightly upwards. It might be attractive, but she would have preferred it otherwise.

She heard someone drop to the deck above and move aft. When she went back to the living quarters, Furse was sitting with Klara with a glass of raspberry and *schnapps* before him.

He got up and came to her and over his shoulder she saw Klara's look, the stolid line of her mouth suddenly softened by the edge of a smile.

She said something and he replied, but the words meant nothing. She saw the cut over his forehead had healed in a thread-fine, dark line.

He had supper with them and played cards for a while afterwards and he was pleasant and made Klara laugh, and all the time she had the feeling that all his talk was for her, that he knew what was happening inside her.

When he went, she walked with him down the length of the foredeck. The river was a smooth band of silk, sprigged with a little pattern of reflected stars. He turned in the shadow thrown by the dock wall behind him and she heard the faint hiss of his cigarette end as it dropped into the water behind him. He put out his hands and held her elbows. She felt her body stiffen and tremble and she thought of the times she had been kissed before and told herself swiftly that this was no more. Then he pulled her gently to him and kissed her and in her mind she fought him off, finding a dozen explanations to reduce the moment to the level of others in the past, and losing them and herself as his arms held her and his mouth touched hers again and drove everything from her but a wish for the moment to go on and on . . .

'Goodnight, Constanta.'

'Goodnight.' Her voice was little more than a whisper.

He went up the ladder quickly and walked away, but it was a long time before she moved and went back to the saloon.

He walked round by the main tower with its illuminated clock faces, through the cobbled streets and over the small iron bridges that spanned the canals that ran through the town. He was restless still. As restless as he had been all day. Having to wait for Charlie was an inaction which seemed to overcharge his energies, and make him seek an outlet for his impatience. It was the excitement of having bet heavily on a race and standing watching with irritation the undisciplined manoeuvres of the horses at the starting gate ... He had been glad when Constanta had asked him to the *Zeehond*. And now . . . he had found there more than he had anticipated. It was the devil; and he was not sure whether he cared for it. What could a man do when a woman's eyes held him as Constanta's had done? He tried to shake the image of her from his mind. You can be as tough, as self-sufficient and wary as you like, he thought, but nothing can help you. A woman rows out in a boat to meet you and, whether you know it then, it's a part of your life coming out to you. You can kick it behind you. You can do what you like – but you can't escape it. And that was the hell of it because he had a feeling that this was something which he ought to escape – for her sake, not his. You can kiss and embrace a hundred women and then one day it's no longer what it always has been. And why? In all he'd had less than a couple of hours' conversation with Constanta and even then he had this other thing on his mind ...

'Mr Furse.'

He knew the voice and stopped, and his hand went automatically to his jacket pocket for the Luger.

There was a little laugh, a woman's laugh, and her voice came teasingly, 'There's no need for that.'

He was on the narrow strip of road leading up to the yacht haven. There were lights from the house windows on his right and to his left a rowing-boat was moving about the yacht basin, the water dripping in phosphorescent rings from the blade strokes. Nothing could touch him here. There was too much light, too many people. He turned back three paces to the parked car which he had unseeingly passed.

Elsa Lieven was at the wheel and Rohner was leaning across her. They smiled at him as though the meeting were accidental and pleasurable, two friends who had happened to recognize him, anxious to recall some moment of mutual pleasure that had held them in the past.

'He carries it everywhere now,' Rohner looked at Elsa and laughed. 'You should have carried it in Rotterdam. It would have kept Pieter off. He hates the things.'

'He's a remarkable young man altogether. Were you looking for me?'

'There's nothing else in Dordrecht.' It was Elsa, and where his hand rested on the edge of the door she put up a finger in the dark and was touching him softly. He dropped his hand. Her dark eyes shining in a white, beautifully oval face, an edge of something white showing lacelike at her throat, she looked composed, intelligent and forgiving . . . but she was a million miles from him now.

He said roughly, 'Of the whole bunch of you the only conversationalist I respect is Dekker. What do you want with me?'

'Just to let you know we're around. We want you to get used to the idea.'

'Goodnight—'

'We might all go and have a drink somewhere.' It was Elsa speaking and she put up a hand towards him.

'You're wasting your time,' he said curtly.

'He doesn't want to be friendly,' said Rohner. 'Let's go.'

CHAPTER EIGHT

The next morning Constanta came alongside the *Arletta* in her small motor launch. She had to go down to Willemsdorp on business and invited him to take the trip with her. He accepted gladly. He had the whole day on his hands until Charlie arrived. He suggested, after she had finished her business in Willemsdorp, that they should have a picnic lunch and spend the rest of the afternoon together. Constanta agreed readily.

Below Willemsdorp, at the head of the Hollandsche Diep, they swung away under the great iron bridge into a region of lagoons and sand banks and flat, reed-fringed islands.

Furse kept the launch at open throttle, finding in the speed and the force of the wind against them an exhilaration which matched his excitement.

He watched Constanta as the wind took her dark hair and drew it back so that the firm line of her temple was shown in an unexpected loftiness that gave a statuesque length and beauty to her face.

'Keep just to port of these stakes,' Constanta said. They were going up a narrow channel between two islands. 'When you reach the one with the basket on it swing over towards the wooden jetty.'

She could hear the tightness in her voice, and knew that it came from a wish not to show too openly the happiness she felt in this man's company. She put out her hands and took the wheel from him.

'Give me. This is tricky and I know the way.'

He edged over and she slid across to take the wheel. She could feel the length of his thigh against her.

They went in past the jetty and the narrow, reed-choked mouth of an old cut opened up. She took the launch down a lane of water, the reeds bending over them and the feathery seeds shaking down on to their clothes. There was a sudden warm smell of grass and blossom. They were in a great pool whose sloping grass banks came down to a thin edge of sand. Beyond the grass was a little stone embankment from behind which old apple trees lifted their heads to watch the water.

They walked through the orchard, across the island to a small cottage where they bought a large white-hearted lettuce to eat with their cheese. Coming back Furse took her hand and they talked, but not about themselves. For the moment they could only trust themselves with the things around them.

After lunch they lay on the grass. Furse watched her. She was lying with her eyes wide open, staring up at the twisted branches of the apple tree. A leaf had fallen, resting in her hair, and her hand lay on the grass holding his.

He said, 'You haven't any lipstick today.'

'You don't like me without it?'

'I like you – any way.'

He bent over and kissed her. She gave her mouth to him and the warmth of her body was against him. He felt the tightening of her fingers in his hair and under his own hands the awakening in her flesh which passed to his own body. His mouth moved over her throat, taking the softness and warmth of her skin. Then suddenly he put her from him, knowing that the strength to do it came from the intensity of his feeling for her, from a love which he had to escape for her sake more than his.

She lay against the grass, one leg drawn up bare and brown, her head thrown back, her eyes shut, her arms thrown out so that the thrust of her shoulders against the earth offered the fulness of her breasts to him.

He put his arms round her and held her gently to him. And in that moment he loved her and knew, with bitterness, that he could not take her love. With Elsa it would not have mattered. But with this girl he realized so well what her attitude to him would be if she knew the full truth about him. There was nothing he could do about it. Even now he felt suddenly ashamed. To hold her like this was false . . . he had no right to raise affection in her. This was what a man did to himself, and to others, when ruthlessness and a fierce self-interest drove him along the wrong path. He could not turn back. He had no wish to turn back, but he knew it would be a long time before he reached the comfortable state of careless indifference to his own conscience. He relased her gently.

Constanta looked up at him and smiled. Then, seeing the look on his face, she was suddenly troubled. For a moment she wanted to ask him what was wrong, to encourage him to speak. Then, with an instinctive wisdom, she realized that she must wait for him. She loved him. That was enough. Sooner or later the love between them would impel his trouble into the open. When that happened she would be ready to help . . . to understand.

Charlie was sitting in the cabin waiting for him. For once his linen suit was pressed and neat and he had the air of an eager schoolboy poised on the edge of a treat. A cigarette was waved awkwardly in a broad fat hand and he said almost reproachfully :

'It is an hour, sir, that I wait for you. Luckily I have thoughts to think, so the time is not wasted.'

'Sorry, Charlie – but I've been out for the day.'

'With a girl, no?'

'Who told you?' The last thing he wanted was to be reminded of Constanta. He had to forget her. Ever since he had left her he had been trying to dismiss her from his mind, to convince himself that their relationship was casual and without importance . . . It was hard but it had to be done.

'The yacht-club boatman. He saw you go off with her this morning. But that is your business. Here—' Charlie tossed an envelope across to him. 'For once I feel good, sir. Damn me, you tell me why I don't ever look inside that thing.'

Furse smiled as he poured them drinks, letting the envelope lie on the table for a while.

'Maybe you knew, Charlie, that it wouldn't help you.'

'Maybe. But now you tell me all about it.'

'Yes – but first I've got to make sure.'

Furse got up and reached for the Chart 192 from the rack.

He spread it on the table and pinned it flat. The sight of the chart raised excitement in him. This was why he was in Holland – for this alone. Nothing else mattered. Nothing else must get in the way.

Charlie glanced at the open hatch door and rose.

'You don't want visitors just now.' He bolted the hatch. Sitting down he put a revolver on the bunk cushion at his side. 'There is money in this? A lot of money?'

'Yes.'

'Good. Then we keep our insurance policy close to hand.'

Furse opened the envelope and took out the overlay. With his pencil he carefully marked in the position of the House of the Seven Flies on Krabbensplaat. He could do it accurately for while he had been anchored up there he had taken a couple of cross-bearings, using the cable beacon at Stadschehoeck and the end of Middelharnis jetty as reference points. He put the overlay on the chart so that the cross marked *Zeven vliegen* fell on the position of the house. Slowly he moved the overlay with the house as the centre of a circle. The other two crosses were fixes which he guessed must be marked on the chart. He found them easily. One was the church at Middelharnis and the other the church at Goudswaard on the other side of the river. But he moved the overlay round in a complete circle to make sure that no other two marks on the chart coincided with the crosses. None did. He oriented the overlay again on the House of the Seven Flies and the two churches. The little dotted circle fell to the south-east of the island, just off shore and a little below the point where the mouth of the cut ran up to the house. He made a pencil mark in the centre of the circle through the overlay on to the chart. Charlie watched him over his shoulder.

'Just there,' said Furse as he straightened up and indicating the slight pencil mark on the chart, 'is nearly a quarter of a million pounds' worth of stones waiting to be picked up. They're in a steel deed-box in the cabin of a smallish motor launch which sank there one night in November 1944. All we have to do is to pick them up and get rid of them quietly.

From what I know of the place the launch can't be lying in more than two fathoms. That means at low tide I could just strip and do the job myself. Maybe, if there's a lot of sand silted into the launch, we'll have to have a diving suit. Could you arrange that?'

Charlie did not say anything for a moment. He puffed awkwardly at his cigarette, his face owlish with thought. Then he picked up the overlay and put a match to it. He held it in his fingers until it had burned away.

'We don't want this now, but to keep it would put temptation in the way of a man like Rohner, say. For a quarter of a million I can arrange anything. These stones are uncut?'

'Mostly.'

'That makes it easier. But in placing them we shall lose on it. Half that amount. Even so it is enough to make a kind of weakness in the stomach when thinking about it. Maybe I like another drink.'

Furse gave him a drink. Charlie went on :

'You sure this is one thing you want to do? A little smuggling . . . these days that is forgivable and a man don't have no trouble with his conscience. For me, with this, I don't have no conscience. That is something I lose when my voice breaks. But how about you?'

Furse shrugged his shoulders. 'Don't worry about me.'

'OK. But I have to ask that question. Once I use you without saying anything. That was wrong and I have a bad feeling, sir. Now – I don't want no more bad feelings. We go in and we go through. Now you tell me all about it.'

'All right. Here goes.'

Furse told him the whole story from the moment Sluiter had come aboard the *Arletta*. How the man had died – and he had gone through his papers. In the briefcase he had found a report of the robbing of the bank. But after Kapitan Walter Maserling had left Dordrecht no other trace of him had been found. Sluiter had worked on the case when he had been employed by the Allied Commission, and after a time the case had been dropped. But later, Sluiter had got hold of a file of official German Naval signals which had put

Sluiter on to Maserling and he had taken up the trail again privately. Sluiter had discovered that Maserling had been made a prisoner of war at the beginning of 1945. He was sent to a camp in England, where he had died of pneumonia. Sluiter's trip to England had been to visit the camp. He had found it disbanded but had discovered that Maserling had made friends with a farmer in the district, almost become one of the family, and that they still had papers belonging to him. Amongst the papers was the chart and the overlay and a letter written to a friend in Germany, but never posted, telling him the full story of the treasure, except the location of the Seven Flies, and asking for his help in what he referred to as 'the Haringvliet project' when he was repatriated. He had never been repatriated or sent the letter. Pneumonia had taken him.

'There were only three things to indicate that Sluiter had been successful in England. The chart, the overlay, and Maserling's letter on which Sluiter had made quite a few notes of his own. I destroyed everything except the overlay. But although he was a careful man, Elsa must have guessed he had found what he wanted. She wanted it, too – but at the last moment she must have been clumsy and scared him and he left her. He was unlucky inasmuch as she had already done the first part of her job – tampered with his insulin supplies. It's not going to be easy to bring this off without interference from Rohner.'

'I can handle him. That is for me. But there is one thing I still don't understand. What about this girl Constanta Straatsma who comes out to meet Sluiter when you get to Veere?'

Furse stood up. For the last half-hour he had forgotten Constanta completely. Being reminded of her now was uncomfortable.

'I don't know,' he said a little harshly. 'She says Sluiter was inquiring about spare marine engine parts for her. Molenaar said the same. It could be true. There doesn't seem any other way she could fit in . . .'

'She is the girl you were with today?'

'Yes.'

'You like her?'

Furse turned quickly. 'What the hell are you getting at, Charlie?'

Charlie made a pacifying motion with his hand and smiled, a sad, tender smile. 'All right – you don't have to bite head off. Can I help it if I am so full of friendliness to you that I take an interest? You spend a day with her, sir. You come back aboard here with a quarter of a million pounds practically in your pocket, but in your eye is something else. What Mama calls it I will not say, for Mama is coarse at times. But I got a right to know. I don't like to do business with a man who might give up all that chance of so much money for a good woman.'

'I'm not giving up any money.'

'Good. When you see her again?'

'Not again. It was a day's outing and it's over. What the hell is this, Charlie?'

'Nothing. I just like to know.'

They both of them laughed and then Charlie went on.

'Now we make a plan. I stay with you tonight, and tomorrow we go up and take a look at this place. First thing we must find out is can you do it alone or do we need a diving outfit.'

After supper Charlie went off to do some telephoning. Furse sat on deck smoking. It was a windless, balmy evening and there was a great peace over the yacht haven. He had an absurd desire to get up and go along to the *Zeehond*, an illogical need to see and be near Constanta again. At all costs he had to avoid that. He couldn't see her again. That would be weakening and he knew just how far he could trust himself. With any other woman, and without the same depth of feeling, he could have worked out a compromise. But not with this girl. The only solution was to cut her out altogether. Up there in the Haringvliet, the tide was sluicing at this moment over a quarter of a million pounds' worth of stones. It was waiting there for him and he was going to have it. No woman was worth a quarter of a million. Although he knew that was how it must be, he could find little comfort in the decision. It was better not to think about her at all. He was glad when Charlie came back, smoking a stubby cigar and carrying a smoked eel.

'This damned corned beef of yours don't make friends with my stomach. Tomorrow I make smoked eel sandwiches.'

CHAPTER NINE

It was just after midday when Rohner overtook them. They were heeling over to a steady east breeze and running down from Willemstad towards the low point of Tien Gemeten. There was a lot of traffic on the river and the air was full of the low thud-thud of barge engines. But beyond Willemstad most of the traffic swung off to the east down the Hellegat. As Furse pointed the *Arletta* up to make the port-hand buoys that followed the line of Beierland, a motor launch came up behind them with a tidy little moustache of white froth at its bows.

'Visitors,' said Charlie who was watching it through the glasses. 'It's the kind of launch you hire by the week in Rotterdam. I make a bet – twenty guilders to one – Rohner has white trousers and a yachting cap.'

'Nothing doing – you've picked him up already in the glasses.'

'True,' Charlie sighed. 'Why can't I ever get anyone to take me on a certainty.'

The *Yssel* came up with them and for a while throttled down to run abreast. They looked a pleasant enough party, Furse thought. Rohner, in a yachting cap, blue blazer and white flannels, was sitting in a cane chair on the forward deck. Elsa sat beside him, her hair blowing in the wind, wearing a white sweater and pale blue linen trousers. On the deck at Rohner's feet lay Pieter, stripped to a pair of tights. At the wheel was Anselm Dekker. He looked more miserable and out of place than Furse had ever seen any man look. He gave a quick glance across at Furse and then turned his head away.

Rohner raised a hand and waved to them and across the five yards of water shouted : 'We're going into Hellevoetsluis for the night. If you get that far come aboard and have a drink. I'll open up a special bottle for you.'

'What of? Poison?' Furse shouted back.

Elsa smiled and Furse saw a frown flash across Rohner's face. He turned and said something to Dekker and the cruiser opened up and passed them.

Furse stood the *Arletta* over towards the Vuile Gat until the cruiser was out of sight, then he put down the helm and ran before the wind, westwards, along the bottom of Tien Gemeten and out into the Haringvliet.

They ran along in the lee of Tien Gemeten and then there was Krabbensplaat coming up over their starboard bow. Furse lowered the mainsail on the *Arletta* and under head-sails went quietly down on the tide which had just started to ebb. They were going to do nothing today which would help Rohner in any way.

'Take the wheel,' he said to Charlie, 'and keep her as she's going.' He went below and got the lead.

Fifty yards below the mouth of the cut he began to take soundings and kept going until they were well beyond the cut. There were between three and three and a half fathoms all the way. With the tide only just beginning to ebb that meant that at low water there would be between eleven and fourteen feet of water. Giving the sunken launch a five-foot clearance above the bed of the river that meant there would be at the most little more than nine feet of water to dive through and, at the best, six. It would be easy.

He coiled the line and when he came up it was to see the *Yssel* idling at the head of the Vuile Gat off the northern end of Krabbensplaat where the Haringvliet joined it.

He sat down by Charlie at the wheel.

'It's a job for low tide. It's four o'clock now and the tide's going. That means dead low about ten tonight. We could come out in the dinghy.'

'No. We can't get rid of Rohner so easily.' Charlie was smoking his cigar and watching the cruiser in the distance. 'You listen to me, sir. This is how we do it. We go into Helle-voetsluis tonight and keep Rohner happy. I'll phone Mama to come and join us and she comes aboard seen by no one. Tomorrow we go out and Mama wears some clothes of yours. She has the build. As soon as Rohner comes past us and gets ahead we slip you and the dinghy off astern and you go away and work all day locating the wreck. Mama and I will sail on. Whenever Rohner comes too near she can go below. In the evening you run the dinghy into Middelharnis and come over on the ferry and walk aboard. Next morning you go off early on the ferry. I lie on deck and the *Arletta* never goes out. Rohner won't know what to do. If you can't pick the stuff up in two days, sir, well, damn me, then we have to have a diving outfit and think of something else.'

'It sounds all right. But we'll have to work it out carefully. If I located the stuff tomorrow I could take the dinghy ashore on Krabbensplaat and wait for the low tide about eleven that evening and maybe pick the stuff up there and then. It depends how much silting has gone on and how the launch is lying.'

'We work it all out. This is a problem for minds like ours. One thing is certain, you must work quietly on it while I lead Rohner the dance. To sail the *Arletta* is easy. I can do that, sir, though I know you hate other people to have her. But it must be. To dive for the stones – that I don't do since I can't swim.'

They were in Hellevoetsluis by five o'clock. Rohner had gone through the lock and tied up in the Vorne canal. Furse came alongside the baulks of timber outside the lock and made fast as Charlie put the fenders out. It was not a good place to lie as he had learned already, but he was anxious to keep as far away from Rohner as possible.

He was stowing the mainsail while Charlie squared up the gear on deck when a voice called to him from the quayside.

'I shouldn't bother to do that, Mr Furse.'

He looked up, his mouth full of sail tiers, and saw Molenaar standing there. A little behind him were two men in uniform, the uniform of the Dutch Customs service.

Furse took the bands from his mouth and said slowly: 'Why not?'

'Because you won't be staying the night here.'

Molenaar dropped on to the deck and, as Charlie came aft, gave him a friendly nod.

Charlie looked from Molenaar to the two Customs men on the quay. 'When people like you look so happy, I don't feel good.'

Furse said, 'I'm still waiting to know why I'm not going to be allowed to stay the night here?'

Molenaar rubbed the nails of his right hand on his jacket lapel and answered quietly, 'Maybe we should go below where we can talk privately. Charlie had better come, too, because this matter concerns him.'

Molenaar stood waiting for them to move, a bulky, well-dressed figure in his brown suit and perfectly knotted brown bow-tie. For a moment Furse felt a touch of anxiety, then, his mind racing over the past few days, he could find no cause for worry. He had done nothing wrong, never given himself away . . . He went across to the companion-way and swung himself down into the cabin.

'Let's have it,' said Furse.

'You two are up to something, and I have a sufficient regard for both of you not to want to be forced to deal with you *after* a crime has been committed.'

Furse said sharply, 'I'm a yachtsman who happened to bring a dead body into this country and I've been told not to leave until the police give me permission. I don't see how I've qualified for this.'

'No? Then I will tell you, Mr Furse. I have had a report on you from the English authorities. There is no actionable evidence against you, but there is ample reason to suppose that for some time you have been smuggling goods into England.'

'He accuses us of smuggling!' Charlie rolled his eyes.

Molenaar ignored and went on, 'I intend to prevent you from getting into trouble – in this country at least – whether from smuggling or other causes . . .' He paused a moment. Furse's face was still, creased at the mouth corners with hard lines. He went on, 'The water-tank on this boat has a false compartment. I discovered it the morning you went off with

117

Miss Straatsma. You also have on board a Luger revolver for which you hold no licence either from us or the English police. Your only contacts in Holland are – pardon me, Charlie – undesirable : Charlie, here, and Mr Rohner and his friends. I am not going to be so simple as to ask you to explain all this. I am informing you – officially – that the Netherlands Government are of the opinion that they don't want you in this country and you are requested to leave.'

'You can tell the Netherlands Government that their request is refused !' Furse said quickly.

'In that case a telephone call will bring an official expulsion order. But I think you will not want me to go as far as that. For your own good you will be leaving this country within the next two hours. There is a good weather report for the North Sea crossing. You have time to fill up with water, petrol and supplies. Until you leave you will have two Customs officers aboard and, when you leave, a Customs launch will escort you to the mouth of the river.'

'And what about me?' asked Charlie.

'You stay here, Charlie. We should hate you to leave the country, because we want you here against the time when we shall catch up on you.'

Furse lit a cigarette and then went and sat on the companion-way steps.

'You know—' he frowned at Molenaar, '—it seems to me that for once the police are getting out of their depths. Here we are, according to you, a couple of smugglers and you warn us off – just at the moment when you've learned about my water-tank and could tip the English water guards off. Somehow, that doesn't seem the moment to hold back. It's not the way policemen behave. There's some other reason and I don't think it's one you want to admit. Don't misunderstand me. I'll go back to England. I haven't any alternative. But I'll never believe you're sending me off because you want to save me from smuggling, to save me from myself. Why aren't you frank with me?'

Molenaar drummed his fingers on the cabin table for a

while, thinking. Even now he was not certain. Furse was quite right, of course. The smuggling was an excuse.

'No, I haven't been frank with you. But then you haven't been frank with me, Mr Furse.'

'Anyone who is frank with a policeman wants his head examined,' sighed Charlie. 'But why do we waste time with talk? You must go to England. I stay here. So.' He made a motion to rise but Furse waved him down.

'You're worrying about Sluiter still?' Furse put the question to Molenaar.

'Yes. I'm worrying about him.'

'You think I had something to do with his death?'

'No. If I did I should not send you back to England. But I am worrying that you know more than you have told me about Sluiter – and particularly about his mission in England. Either you know about that or you don't. If you don't, then you won't know what I'm talking about. If you do . . .' Molenaar stood up as he spoke, 'then get this quite clear. I'm kicking you out of the Netherlands because I don't intend that you shall get your hands on a lot of easy money. It's the only way open to me.'

'What is all this easy money you're talking about?' Furse said it easily, with just that edge of puzzled curiosity in his voice that was needed, but he felt the rising stir of anger and frustration in himself. Suddenly, everything had blown up in his face.

'If you don't understand what I'm talking about,' said Molenaar, 'then it doesn't matter.'

'We don't understand you,' said Charlie. 'But OK. Mr Furse is to go – and that's that.'

'You can get your things together, Charlie, and leave now,' said Molenaar, moving towards the companion-way. 'Two hours, Mr Furse. You can go ashore, do anything you like as far as stores are concerned, but I'm sure you won't mind if I insist that a Customs man goes with you.'

Charlie moved forward to get his bag while Furse went up on deck with Molenaar. They stood there waiting for Charlie and neither of them spoke. The two Customs men stood on the quay and behind them was a pale gold line of evening cloud. A handful of terns came swirling into the harbour mouth, dropping delicately into the water now and again as they fished. It was going to be a wonderful evening, Furse thought. A lovely evening to begin a crossing, to begin the long journey home with his hands empty.

Charlie came up on deck, his case in his hand. He looked ruffled and bad-tempered, like a battered old crow, but there was a bright glint in his eyes.

'What a country, damn me. Why don't you send me away, too? It would be a pleasure. A man tries to keep his nose clean and somebody accuses him of stealing handker-chiefs. Captain, sir, you don't let this lose you your sleep or appetite.' He put a hand on Furse's arm, 'I don't take my smoked eel. You finish him tonight.'

'Come on, Charlie.' Molenaar moved impatiently.

'OK.'

'Goodbye, Charlie,' said Furse. 'See you in some other country, some time.'

He watched them move across the quay and then one of the Customs men came aboard and settled himself in the stern where he began to fill a pipe.

CHAPTER TEN

Two hours were more than enough. He had filled his water and petrol tanks at Dordrecht that morning before leaving and for food he had plenty of corned beef and biscuits. The Customs man helped him haul his dinghy aboard and lash it securely.

A little while before he was ready to sail Rohner and Elsa came strolling down the quay. They stood watching him while he bent a storm jib to take the place of the summer canvas he had been carrying in the rivers. Rohner came over to the quay edge and said :

'You've created a sensation, Mr Furse. Everyone knows you're being sent back. Bad luck.'

The Customs man came along the deck and gave Rohner a frown.

'It is forbidden to speak to the English captain. You will go, please.'

'Don't worry,' said Furse. 'I don't want to speak to him.' He turned his back on Rohner and heard Elsa's light laugh. Behind him he heard Rohner again :

'Don't worry, Mr Furse. I will write to you in England, or maybe come and see you—'

'Mynheer – you want that I should order you off the quay?' It was the Customs officer and there was an ugly note in his voice.

It wanted half an hour to eight o'clock when he took the *Arletta* out. The Customs man stayed aboard. A Customs launch which had been lying in the tramway harbour now preceded the *Arletta* out into the river.

Under the light beacon at the entrance to the harbour Furse saw Molenaar and Charlie standing. Molenaar raised a hand in a statuesque, vaguely antique farewell and Furse smiled to himself as he imagined the triumph which the man was feeling. Charlie, alongside Molenaar, gave an expressive hunch of his shoulders and flapped his arms helplessly.

Outside the tide was sluicing strongly seawards and, as Furse put the helm over to run with it, he saw a barge coming up from the direction of Tien Gemeten. The yellow and black paint of the deck-house was familiar and picking up his glasses he focused on the craft. Almost at once he had Constanta in view. She was standing on the port bow, swaying a little to the motion of the barge, her hands in her pockets and a red scarf flying from her neck. He put the glasses down quickly.

'Take the wheel,' he said to the Customs man. 'I'll get some sail on her.'

He went forward, but Constanta's face was clear in his mind, a long beautiful oval, the soft brilliance of her half-parted lips and the dark depths of her eyes . . . He swore to himself and pushed the image from him as he ran up the jib.

He was going back to England, back to Jimmy, and the unpleasant certainty that there would never be any more easy money from Charlie in Holland. What the hell was he to do? Charter parties couldn't keep a boy at a public school and a man in cigarettes and whisky. The only thing he could do was to sell the *Arletta* and go cap in hand to some friend and cadge for a nine-till-six job.

At the wheel he looked up and saw the burgee standing out stiff and brave, and there was a ring of tidy white curls around the bare sand banks. There was a good moderate breeze and she was heeling over pleasantly, making the water hiss under her counter, shaking herself now and then as though she were glad to be getting out to sea again, anxious to wash off the footing of river mud and oil around her. The swift, bubbling call of sandpipers suddenly swept down on him with the wind and somehow he knew that the moment he lost the *Arletta* he would have lost himself.

The Customs man lit a pipe, sitting alongside him, and said :

'She is a good boat. By midday tomorrow you will be home.'

'Yes.' He was in no mood for talking.

Above Hellevoetsluis the launch swung over to the Goeree side of the river and stayed with him, leading the way through the buoyed channel of the Slijkgat until he was over the Hinder Bank and at sea about twelve miles from Hellevoetsluis. It was ten o'clock, almost dark and dead low tide when the Customs launch came alongside. There was hardly any sea running and the man from the *Arletta* was taken aboard the launch easily.

Five minutes later and the lights of the launch were fading into the east and Furse was alone. He kept on his course until the lights were gone and then hove-to.

He lit a cigarette and sat with his arm crooked over the wheel. The *Arletta* was riding easily, her gear complaining gently as now and again she fell away from the wind and then came swinging back. Sea and sky had merged into an uneven darkness. Overhead a few uncertain stars pricked through the shabby blackness like light through a worn carbon sheet.

Well, he told himself – this is it. Somewhere in the Haringvliet were the stones and that was where they would go on lying for a long time. It was a situation he could not accept. If only . . . If only he could get back and lift the stuff himself. It was a project full of risks. Just thinking about it raised a quick pulse of excitement in him. But how the hell could a man do it? He was due in England the following evening. Molenaar would check on his arrival – but until then no one would know where he was. If he slipped back with the tide tonight and lay up in the pool at Krabbensplaat he would have the following day to make a bid for the stones. If he were lucky he could come out on the tide that night . . . After that he could make for Ostend or some other port and find a place to hide them and then take his own time before he went across . . . He had only been asked to leave Holland. There was no law against his loitering down the Channel coast. For a while he played with the idea. The trouble was he could never do it alone. If only he could have had a word with Charlie and arranged for him to be at Krabbensplaat the next morning.

He went below to get himself some supper. Coffee and smoked eel, he decided. He went to the galley and got down the tin in which Charlie had put the eel. As he opened the lid he saw that there was a sheet of notepaper on top of the brown coil of eel. He took it under the cabin lamp and read it.

Captain, sir. Take the biggest risk when they least expect it. Tonight I stay in Ferry Hotel, Hellevoetsluis. Come back on tide. Ring me morning from Krabbensplaat. You can do it – with me.

It was all he needed. Charlie had taken the opportunity which had been denied to him. There was a telephone at the House of the Seven Flies. That he had learned from Beukleman. He reached up and got his charts and the North Sea Pilot, Part IV. Going in at night without lights would not be easy, particularly as he was not too familiar with the channels. It would be simple to go wrong and find himself aground. There was one consolation, however. He would be going in on a rising tide. His one danger was being caught. If Molenaar got hold of him the man's temper would change. He could tell the truth, but that meant explaining about Rohner and he had not forgotten Rohner's threat to implicate him ... Even without that there would be plenty of trouble. But against all this, there was a rising confidence in him. With Charlie and a bit of luck it could be done.

He went up and doused his navigation lights.

In Hellevoetsluis, Constanta and Klara were sitting outside the wheel-house. It was a warm night. Klara was knitting and Constanta lay back in her deck-chair, her hands behind her head, watching the pale-winged moths that fluttered about the electric bulb over the door. Now and again Klara looked across at her curiously. She knew Constanta well enough to realize that the girl was worrying about something, and she had a shrewd idea that it was nothing to do with her business.

It was an hour since Molenaar had left Constanta. He had seen her barge come in and had been waiting for her. He had told her the action he had taken with Furse and Constanta had been careful to keep back any expression of her own feelings. It would have served no purpose to tell him that she had deliberately altered her barge schedule to follow Furse to Hellevoetsluis simply because, since her outing with him, she had come to the decision that the thing which was holding them apart was the fact that Furse was trying to take the Bank's stones. In her own mind she kept to the word 'take' rather than 'steal'. An idea had grown in her that if she could see him again and talk to him about it, tell him the truth about her own relationship with Sluiter, he might be honest with her and she might be able to persuade him to drop a project to which, some instinct told her, he was not entirely committed in his heart.

'I think,' she said suddenly, 'that I will have a letter from him soon.'

Klara did not ask her of whom she was speaking. She knew.

'He is a man to forget,' she said severely, her needles bickering gently, and there was an angry tenderness in her voice.

'I don't want to forget him.' From a child, Klara had known that stubborn note in Constanta's voice.

'It is better that we talk of something else. You think it is good that I should encourage you to think about a man who is a smuggler, a rogue and a thief and who associates with such people? . . .' She made an angry little sound. But, glancing at Constanta, she knew that the girl was in love, and when you were like that it was no help having common sense thrown at you. The thing had to run out of its own accord.

Constanta got up and went on to the quay. Klara, she felt, would only end by annoying her from the best of motives. She walked up towards the town slowly. The man had kissed her, wanted to feel as she had felt and then, abruptly, everything had collapsed between them. And she knew why. The other thing held him back. It was her sureness of this which gave her hope. She could not mistrust a man whose behaviour towards her had been so controlled by decency. It might be illogical, but because of this she felt that he could never be a thief. He was alone, things hadn't gone well with him since the war, perhaps there was a weakness in him . . . But he only wanted someone to bully him, to point out vigorously the stupidity he was building around himself . . .

Because she had no desire to go back and have to talk to Klara and Oom Paul, she turned into the Ferry Hotel to dine by herself. Her thoughts and speculations about Furse were all the company she needed at this moment. She had been sitting at her table for some time before she realized that Charlie Ponz was also in the room. He was eating at a table near the window. Molenaar had pointed him out to her and told her of his association with Furse.

Charlie was eating an omelette and drinking *aquavite*. In imagination he was out off the Hinder Bank now with Furse. A quarter of a million pounds, less expenses. Damn me – for that amount of money a man should do a little thinking, take a few risks. All Furse would need was the right touch. He sat back, lit himself a cigarette and offered up a prayer that the touch he had left in the smoked eel box would come to his notice. The damn fool might be quite likely to go without supper.

He paid his bill and went across to Constanta. He had seen her the moment she had entered the room. He stood smiling by her table and said :

'Good evening, miss. Captain Furse gave me his kind regards for you before he left. It is a pity the police make such a big mistake with his reputation. For me, I think he could start a libel action, or maybe I mean slander.' He pulled a card from his breast pocket and dropped it on the table. 'Ever you want something in Rotterdam, that's me. Cheap nylons, coffee, some business rival fixed, a quick passage somewhere without passport . . . you just look me up.' The smile broadened and one eye flickered gently in a wink. 'Now, I must get back to Rotterdam.'

'Thank you,' said Constanta, picking up the card. She found herself liking this bright little man and she was tempted to hold him, to talk to him about Furse. But all she said was, 'You're going back to Rotterdam tonight?'

Charlie spread his hands and his lips pouted. 'Why not? Is there anything to keep me here? I don't think of nothing.'

Outside Charlie began to stroll down towards the river. The wind had eased almost to a calm and there were patches of high misty cloud drifting across the pale stars. She was a nice girl, he thought. Just the kind of nice girl that made a man do rash things like trying to be worthy of her.

On Rohner's launch both Dekker and Pieter were asleep forward. Rohner and Elsa were sitting in the stern under a canvas canopy with scalloped edges. On the table between them were glasses, cigarettes and a bottle of Bols. They were arguing, both keeping their voices low, like parents afraid of waking the children, both trying to force the other to a decision and both knowing that in the end Elsa would gain her point. Both of them knew that their only hope now lay in Charlie and persuading him to work with them. Their difference of opinion lay in deciding whether they should go to Charlie or wait until he came to them.

Rohner, impatient, wanted to go to him. But Elsa knew that it would be better to wait until he came to them. It would give them a bargaining advantage which, in dealing with Charlie, was almost essential. To neither of them did it occur that Charlie might not want any help from them.

Molenaar was having supper with the captain of the Customs patrol cutter. Molenaar had no feeling for the sea and no enthusiasm for ships, and the prospect of spending the night patrolling the mouth of the river was unattractive. But he was a policeman and used to working against his own inclinations.

Furse had gone, but Molenaar's suspicions of the man

remained. He remembered his conversation with his chief and the case of the Frenchman Delacroix. He had learned a lesson there which he intended to profit by this time. You can kick a man out of a country, but that is no guarantee that he will not try to come back if the incentive is strong enough. A quarter of a million pounds was enough incentive for any man.

The captain, seeing that he was eating little, said, 'You need not be afraid to make a good supper. It will not be rough tonight – and, even if it should be, it is always better to have a good cargo aboard so that you have something to jettison. You think this man will try to come back?'

'I don't know. We can only wait and see. If he does and we get him – then life is going to be uncomfortable for him.'

'So. Then in an hour we leave. If he comes he will take the tide.'

CHAPTER ELEVEN

He came in with the tide, ghosting along under the jib. Running into the river mouth was easy for he had the leading lights first from Westhoofd and then from Kwade Hoek on the northern end of Goeree island. Once he was in the river the trouble would start.

He went in without lights except for the luminous pallor of the binnacle which he had half draped with a handkerchief. Time went by in a slow, unmarked stream. He stood, lifting and swaying gently to the movement of the *Arletta*, stood there for an age, boring steadily into the night. By the time he made the mouth of the river he was keyed up and his hands were soft with sweat. He switched off the binnacle light and checked his course now and again with a hand torch, the details of his chart and the pilot book instructions clear in his mind. There were buoy lights down the river, but he knew he would not be able to hold them rigidly for the channel twisted and swerved. For all he knew there might be a Customs patrol in the river mouth. That would mean he would have to leave the normal channels. The thought of doing this with the tide so low made him swear gently to himself. He was crazy. Absolutely bloody crazy . . . but it was the kind of craziness you had to have if you wanted to pick up a quarter of a million. He thought of Jimmy, asleep in his dormitory now, and it started a complexity of thoughts that harassed him and he shut them from his mind.

He was in the river now, peering into the darkness trying to pick out the slow loom of a sand bank emerging from the darkness in a dull spread of paleness, hearing the deceptive sound of breaking water, concentrating on distance, checking his watch, his binnacle and the fixed memory of his chart, seeing the *Arletta* as a black speck that moved slowly across the white and grey spaces of the chart. He went in, clinging to the tide, letting it take him and waiting for the ghost-like shapes of the buoys to swim up to him out of the darkness.

On his port hand he suddenly heard the bubbling night-cry of curlews and, as though the dark face of the waters had been rubbed thin and bare, he saw a blowing line of foam scuds at the edge of a bank. He swung the wheel over. But it was too late. The *Arletta* bumped gently two or three times. A swift panic swept through him. He heard the sudden boiling of water astern as the tide pushed at her and she faltered, reluctant to leave the sand.

He started the motor, slammed it into reverse, and the night was broken with the sudden roar of the engine. He gave the motor full throttle. With a clumsy shudder, the *Arletta* came off. Slowly he edged back into the main channel. As soon as he was clear, he switched off the motor. If there were a patrol boat about the noise of his engine had been thudding across the water like a tom-tom for them to hear. He cursed himself for running aground. He knew what had happened. He had swung too far over to starboard and run close to the great Scheelhoek bank that sprawled half across the inside of the mouth of the river. Lower down, and almost abreast of Hellevoetsluis, was another bank, the Slijk-plaat dead in the middle of the stream. He would have to leave that on his port hand, keeping the bank between himself and Hellevoetsluis.

Back in the mainstream, his course checked on the compass and the distant light at Hellevoetsluis just coming up over his port bow, he found himself cold and curiously limp from his escape.

The night lapsed to a gentle susurration of sounds. He reached for a cigarette, blaming himself still for the necessity of having to start his motor. His hand was on his matches when he knew that the harm had been done. Astern of him and on the far side of the river, he heard the abrupt burst into life of a powerful marine engine and a small searchlight drew a swift band of silver across the water behind him. He ducked and saw the deck of the *Arletta* come up out of darkness in a hard pattern of grey and silver. The searchlight wheeled away from him, lifting and probing and then swung back, breaking over him in a cruel dazzle of light and was past him so swiftly that he prayed he had not been seen. The light, almost as though it were human, suspecting it had outraced itself and left unmarked its quarry, wavered on his port side a hundred yards away and then began to creep slowly back. Each moment its path drew nearer, and each moment, as the Customs cutter came downstream, the funnel of light widened . . . The patrol boat, Furse judged, was about half a mile away and overhauling him rapidly.

He had only one course; to start his motor. He opened up his engine, its beat muffled now by the sound of the other boat, and drew away ahead, sheering towards the southerly side of the river. The light came creeping slowly back towards him. He could see the scuffle of foam from his wake sliding under its beam. In a few moments it would be up with him. Then, as despair and anger began to move in him, the light suddenly jerked upwards, arched the night sky in a magnificent sweep and dropped in a still line with a faint halo of the northern bank marking its far end. Slowly it began to work round across the river towards him again. The patrol boat was now close enough for him to make out the red and green navigation lights. It was dead astern of him with the light lying off at an angle of ninety degrees from its port bow and gradually traversing towards him. He thought of the man behind that beam, his visual world narrowed to a ranging funnel of silver and grey shapes, of Molenaar who was possibly aboard and who had been suspicious enough to foresee that he might come back . . . of Charlie waiting over in Hellevoetsluis, this same searchlight probably throwing wheeling shadows on his bedroom ceiling, and of all the chances he had let pass to back out of this affair . . . But he was in now, in deep and desperately and a spasm of angry courage stirred through him at the thought of failure. He had to make it, had to get to Krabbensplaat and take the chance of twenty-four hours in which to prove the risk. He would want luck to take him through and he knew that luck never worked for him unless he threw overboard all doubts and fears. In that moment, although he knew he had been and still was a fool, he was suddenly clear-headed and determined. Nothing was going to stop him.

Out of the grey pallor of the disturbed night, a great shape suddenly loomed up just off his port bow. There was the sound of angry water tearing against the side of a large buoy and as he went by he caught the initials AG-HV painted on it. He knew at once where he was, at the seaward tip of the long Slijkplaat bank, but he should have passed the buoy on his starboard hand. The set of the tide where the channel divided had driven him too far north. He swung the *Arletta* over to starboard and prayed there would be enough water now to take him over the tip of the bank, his mind photographing the section of the chart that showed the tear-drop shape of the outer shallows of the bank.

It was at this moment that the searchlight caught him. The deck works and rigging of the *Arletta* blazed with light points. He thought he heard a shout behind him, faint across the water, and he was overwhelmed with a strange sense of standing suddenly naked in a hostile world, his shadow leaping, elongated and macabre, before him.

He spun the wheel and broke from the light, but in a second it was back on him. He opened up the motor and went twisting and curving away from it. Each time he escaped it came back, holding him until he began to have the odd impression that it was not the light which came to him, but he who fought and twisted to find the light, held and impelled by it like a moth before a candle flame.

How long the chase went on he had no idea. Time, as in a dream, lost all significance. There was only himself, cold and angry, spinning the wheel, flashing in and out of two worlds, one dark and oppressive, filled with the roar of his own engine, the other cruelly bright with his own shadow dancing ahead of him and the *Arletta* leaping forward like a ghost ship. Once he glanced over his shoulder and the great beam of light struck his face as though it dealt a physical blow.

The end came suddenly. There was a slight bump. The

Arletta rose gracefully like a living creature. Another bump and then a long succession of harsh grating noises against her keel and an agonizing series of shudders that vibrated through her hull as though some unseen power, malicious and frenzied, were hammering at her. He was thrown sideways and felt his face strike the side of the wheel shelter. He pulled himself up, his hand going to his face to come away wet with blood that ran from a cut over his eye. The engine had stalled and, as he stood up, he saw that the *Arletta* was heeled over, well aground. Just off her starboard bow was a long stretch of sand, grey and light-speckled from the searchlight, the long ridges of wave marks from the last tide shadowed across the rising whaleback in a regular dark pattern.

The patrol boat was standing off from him about fifty yards away. He stood there in the full glare of the light, hearing the gentle beat of its motor. Then the light went out and was replaced by a masthead lamp that tilted towards him, a pale, golden glow, wonderfully soft and comforting after the harshness of the searchlight.

'Stay on deck where we can see you. Don't move!' A voice, strange to him, shouted across the water.

Without thought or apprehension he lit a cigarette and watched as a dinghy was slung over the side of the patrol boat. The captain was not risking bringing the cutter any closer to the bank.

Two men dropped into the dinghy and one of them began to row. The boat came across the swing of the tide towards him, crabbing its way, the oars pock-marking the dark current with white eddies. It dropped down on him from astern and he leaned over and took the painter which Molenaar handed him while the Customs man shipped oars and steadied the dinghy alongside. He made the painter fast and reached out a hand to help Molenaar aboard. He had no animosity towards him, only a quiet alertness and determination.

'You're the biggest bloody fool that ever walked!' snapped Molenaar.

'Yes?' The word was cold, almost insolent.

'Coming back like this! It proves I was right about you!' Seeing Furse standing tall and hard-faced, the blood running down his cheek, Molenaar realized that he had always hoped his suspicions would be proved wrong.

'I decided I wouldn't be kicked around.'

Molenaar made an impatient movement of his hand. 'We'll talk about that later. You'd better get below so we can have a look at that cut on your face.' He put out a hand and pushed Furse towards the hatchway. But as he followed him down he was deciding that he would have to go carefully even now. The man had defied their request, but in itself it was not criminal. On the other hand coming back so secretly lent weight to his suspicions . . . He decided that the best thing to do would be to get him to Hellevoetsluis where he could ring his chief for instructions. The Customs people could take charge of the *Arletta*.

Furse turned the light on and Molenaar dropped to a bunk seat, resting his elbows on the table.

'Get that cut washed up. It looks deep. Then you're coming to Hellevoetsluis. You didn't come back out of defiance. You know that. You came back with a purpose.'

'I came back. Put your own interpretation on it.' Furse went to the galley and drew himself a basin of water. A desperate anger rose in him at the thought of *Arletta* piled up on the sand, and a quarter of a million lost to him for ever. He stood there with the basin of water in his hands and suddenly knew what he must do.

'My interpretation will be the same as a great many other people's when they know the facts.' Molenaar leaned back, shaking his head.

With a quick movement Furse tossed the basin of water into Molenaar's lap. He turned, switched off the saloon light, and was up the hatchway.

He heard Molenaar swear behind him and then he had slammed the hatch cover over and bolted it. He turned and saw the man by the dinghy moving towards him.

'Hey, what the—'

Furse hit him and he went down, rolling across the deck. He leaped to the starboard side of *Arletta*, whipped free the dinghy painter and dropped into the boat. He pushed it off, screened by the bulk of *Arletta*'s hull, and felt the strengthening tide tear him away downstream. As he went he heard Molenaar shouting and beating against the hatch and then an angry call from the man on deck to the patrol boat.

Furse took the oars and in a couple of strong strokes was outside the golden halo of light from the patrol boat into a welcome darkness. He pulled savagely, making the water boil under the dinghy's bows, and headed across the shallows of the slowly submerging Slijkplaat, knowing that the patrol boat would not be able to follow him.

He pulled away into the night, taking the north side of the Slijkplaat. As he did so, he heard a confusion of shouts between the boats behind him. He rowed desperately, anticipating with each movement the cruel stab of the searchlight over the waters. When it came it flashed to his left, and then swung towards him. He crouched low, oars drawn in. It passed over him quickly, failing to pick him up. Savagely he forced the dinghy on and reached the cover of the hump of long sand bank. The light broke over the bank but he passed now safely in its shadow. He pulled with the tide in long steady strokes and, when he reached the end of the bank, swung across southwards to the Overflakkee shore and hugged the shallow water down its length. Behind him he saw the searchlight sweeping and dipping. The patrol boat had gone upstream to clear the shallows and was now hunting along the north bank of the Slijkplaat. After a while it came fast downstream and began to quarter the water below the bank, but by this time he was well away.

He had been lucky, he told himself. But he had worked for his luck. Now it must go on.

It was four o'clock when he made the mouth of the cut at Krabbensplaat and the darkness was thinning. He went in gently to the shore and jumped overboard in a few inches of water. He gave the dinghy a push and saw her float off. The tide took her and she began to move away downstream.

Some time she would be found, but when she was it would be miles from Krabbensplaat.

He dropped on the grass beneath the poplars and lay for a while, relaxed from the strain and exhaustion of the night, shutting all thought from his mind. In a few moments he was asleep and slept until half past five.

When he awoke, the sun was coming up. He stood up and brushed himself down. He washed the dried blood from his face with his handkerchief and then went slowly up towards the house. Beyond the wooden quay he met Jan Beukleman, a basket of duck eggs under his arm, coming from a small paddock of apple trees to one side of the cut. He was in his working clothes, his leather jerkin and patched trousers, and wore clogs on his feet. It was a bright morning and the hardening light gave an ivory gloss to the large face, drawing sharp shadows in the furrowed cheeks. He gave Furse a shy smile as he greeted him and Furse was surprised to find that he had forgotten how dark and lively the man's eyes were.

'So you have come back to us, mynheer?'

For a moment Furse wondered if Beukleman, too, had heard about his being sent away but a glance at the man told him this was not so. His voice was even and friendly.

'Yes. I came over in my dinghy. It's at the mouth of the cut. Do you mind if I have a look around the island today?'

'No, mynheer. Usually I do not encourage people because they wander all over the place. You know how it is. They do damage without meaning to, and they disturb my cattle.' Jan Beukleman paused, a frown of concern shadowing his eyes. 'That's a nasty cut you have on your face.'

'It's nothing. The boom swung over and hit me.'

'My wife must put some plaster on it for you. If you come up to the house . . . You are also in time for breakfast. My wife would be pleased.'

Furse accepted the invitation gladly. He wanted to go to the house, anyway, to telephone. They went through the great wrought-iron gateway with its seven flies into the walled yard with its edging of trim flower beds and each cobble apparently washed and polished.

'Do you mind if I use your telephone? I want to speak to a friend in Hellevoetsluis.'

'You are welcome, mynheer.'

The front door of the house led into a great hall out of which rose a magnificent curved stairway. The floor was slated and a wide open fireplace, bright with blue and white Delf tiles, took up the whole of one wall almost. There was a richness of brown and gold about the place which made Furse think of some of the Dutch paintings he had seen. A highly polished press squatted in the curve of the stairs, ranged with pewter plates; and stiff elaborate chairs stood around a long refectory table, their scarlet velvet faded, their fringes of heavy gold tassels hanging straight and prim. A convex mirror in a gold-gilt frame reflected the room and drew it out until one seemed to be standing in a vast salon; around the walls were oil paintings of women in rich brocades and ruffs, severe lace and stiff head-dresses and of men in sober black cloth and high black hats . . . Looking around Furse had the feeling that nothing in this room had changed in the last hundred years.

Beukleman slid off his clogs and moved quietly across the slates in his felt liners towards a door at the side of the fireplace.

'The telephone, mynheer, is at the foot of the stairs. When you have finished come into the kitchen.'

The telephone, Furse thought, had no place in the room. It was the one false note but he was glad of it. He picked it up gingerly, conscious of its sleek, black polish and the smell of furniture cream that came from it. After a time a man's voice answered him and he asked to be put through to the Ferry Hotel at Hellevoetsluis.

In a few minutes Charlie was on the line.

'Charlie?'

'Captain, sir. Where?' There was a new hardness and intensity in Charlie's voice.

'Seven Flies. Must have a boat.'

'OK. One hour.'

'Be careful.'

'Hell, yes.'

Furse turned away from the telephone, his spirits lifting.

Jan Beukleman and his wife were waiting for him in the kitchen. She was a short, plump woman with a stiff apron tied tightly round her waist, her arms bare and red, the hands thick and capable. Her grey hair was pulled tightly back off her forehead and gathered into a bun at the back. She wore steel-rimmed glasses and said little, but behind the glasses Furse could see the same kind of lively eyes that Beukleman had. Before they ate she insisted on putting some plaster on his cut. They were a nice couple and he liked them and, although there were periods when they were all silent over the meal, he found the silence no embarrassment.

On the table were ham, cheese, rolls and gingerbread and jam. He ate more than he would normally have done to please them and was given a cigar to smoke with his last cup of coffee. When he left them – telling them that he was expecting a friend over from Hellevoetsluis for the day – it was with the invitation to come back and have supper with them.

He walked slowly across the yard in the sunshine and back to the mouth of the cut. It was still not quite seven o'clock and he settled down to finish his cigar and wait for the arrival of Charlie. He lay on the grass and felt the warmth of the sun through his shirt and the feeling for the moment reminded him of the laziness and warmth which had been in him the day Sluiter had come walking across the railway tracks to the *Arletta*. It seemed a long time ago, and somehow the man who had greeted Sluiter that day seemed a different creature from the man who lay on the grass now and watched the blue wraiths of cigar smoke go curling up into the air.

Just after seven he heard the putter of a motor and rose to find a dinghy with an outboard motor coming into the cut. Charlie was at the tiller in his wrinkled linen suit, his thin brown hair ruffled, and a hand raised in greeting.

CHAPTER TWELVE

Charlie sat on the grass by his side and put the whole thing clearly.

'It's all right, sir, whichever way. We have luck and we get this stuff today; well then, we can slip off here tonight and be out of the country by tomorrow. After that the police can say and do what they like. But, damn me, what have they got? Only your boat. You can buy a hundred more. And no proof you did nothing but a mad English trick in coming back because you don't like being booted up the bottom out of here without proper legal procedure.'

'And if we don't have luck?'

'So then? I get you out of the country just the same. Some time later I come back here and you trust me to do the job solus and see you come out all right.'

Furse was far from sure about this. He knew his Charlie and it would be a great temptation for him, if he worked alone, to lift the stones and say nothing about them. He did not blame Charlie for this. That was just Charlie.

'You don't trust me, captain, sir?' Charlie saw his hesitation, and understood it. 'You think if you go and I do this job alone, maybe I never tell you?'

Furse grinned. 'What do you think?'

Charlie was silent for a while, his face drawn with sad lines. Then he said slowly, 'Maybe. I don't trust myself, sir, to know what I would do. But that don't happen. Damn me, we have luck today. Then everything is OK.'

'We've got to have luck today,' said Furse grimly.

It had been high water that morning at six and it was now half past seven. Low water dead was at about one o'clock and that was the best time for diving. They had the morning to locate the sunken launch. They wasted no further time.

They took Charlie's rowing-boat with the outboard motor down to the mouth of the cut and relying on his memory of the chart Furse worked out the probable position of the wreck. It was impossible to be definite, but they roughed out an area about a hundred yards long by fifty wide and fixed it by reference points on the island shore. It was some time before they had this done and could begin searching.

They worked up and down the tide flow, starting on the side of the rectangle farthest away from the island. Charlie was at the tiller operating the motor and one grapple while Furse worked the other. The grapples they had devised for themselves. Charlie had the dinghy anchor on a length of rope and Furse had a large manure rake with long curved prongs that he had quietly taken from Beukleman's yard. The handle of the rake was about eight feet long and to this he had lashed a long pole also borrowed unasked from the yard. The head of the rake he had weighted to keep it down. At full high water he knew there was little more than eighteen feet of water in the area they were searching and as it was now four hours before low tide there was less than this.

The water was too full of sediment for them to be able to see the bottom, which was for the most part a clean run of mud and sand. They worked slowly up and down, Furse feeling the grate and bump of the rake prongs over the bottom, Charlie with the warp in his hand easing and shortening it to keep the feel of the small anchor as it moved draggingly behind the boat. Charlie sat coaxing the motor to its lowest speed and judging his turns at the end of the rectangle to come back into place for the next run, like a ploughman swinging a tractor into the next neat furrow.

It was difficult work and impossible for a man to do alone. If he had come back without Charlie, Furse knew he could not have handled it by himself. Every now and again the anchor or the rake would catch on some underwater obstruction and they hung over the spot, feeling and probing with the rake. Usually it soon became clear that they were over a rock, but once Furse stripped to his trunks to dive into twelve feet of water only to find the water-logged skeleton of a tree bedded in the sand.

There was little traffic on this side of the island. Sometimes a sailing barge came down loaded with hay and a few yachts passed away close to the Overflakkee shore. They kept a sharp look-out and, before anything came too near they ran into the mouth of the cut to hide. It was irritating to have to do this, but it had to be done. Each time it happened Furse felt the impatience growing in him. It had become an urgent conviction with him that they had to find the stones today. If they didn't . . . he never would have any benefit from them and he would be in a mess, without the *Arletta* for months. For all he knew she might have sprung her timbers going aground . . . Today. They had to find the stuff today. The thought went through his head insistently.

The heat shimmer over the water broke the far line of Overflakkee with a pale streak of dancing silver tufted with the floating tops of trees and buildings. Each time they passed the mouth of the cut Furse got a glimpse of the house, its gable fronts marking a bold convolution against the blue sky. They went on with their combing of the water. Furse felt a slow ache beginning to take his back and arms and the drag of the rake seemed to have increased ten times. There was little talk between them, except the orders which he passed to Charlie.

Furse leaned half over the gunwale, the cool water lapping about his wrists as he dragged the pole, the steady beat of the motor drumming into his ears, and the heat of the sun striking at his half-naked body. Suddenly he discovered that he was thinking of Constanta. She was not far away, over in Hellevoetsluis. He wondered if she had heard the news of his return? What would she think about that? What the hell did he care what she thought, anyway? He could say it fiercely – but somewhere deep inside him, he knew he cared.

The motor died and Furse turned to find Charlie braced back against the rope. The boat swung slowly broadside to the stream.

'Something there?'

Charlie nodded. 'I think, maybe, yes.'

He moved over with the rake, the water dripping down on

to him as he swung it. 'Take her round, Charlie, and come back up on it. Pay out as we go round and then take in the slack as we come up.'

Charlie manoeuvred the boat round and as they came back Furse helped to haul in on the rope. When they were almost over the obstruction Charlie throttled the motor down so that they were just stemming the tide. The shore was not fifty yards from them and they were just below the mouth of the cut.

Furse began to probe and feel with the rake. There was something down there.

'What do you think, sir?' Charlie was watching him tensely.

'There's something. I'll go down.' He brought the rake inboard. 'Do you think that anchor will hold?'

'Yes. You go down.' Charlie watched Furse as he lowered himself over the stern. The boat was too small to let him dive without fear of capsizing it.

'Here I go.'

Furse raised his arms and let himself sink. He rolled over and swam down against the strong current. He was in a greenish brown fog that eddied before his eyes. His hands struck against something and the fog was suddenly darker about him. He kicked forward and his fingers were on a run of slippery wood. A swift exhilaration took him and he moved forward, half swimming, half pulling himself, his hands groping in the darkness.

When he came up Charlie looked at him inquiringly. He hung against the boat sucking greedily at the air.

'I don't know,' he said after a moment. 'It may be.'

He went down again, husbanding his breath until he thought his lungs would burst, and this time there was no doubt in his mind. He worked his way over a flat wooden surface and then dropped four feet before he found wood again and knew that he had come over a cabin-top into the well of a small launch. Four times he went down, saying little to Charlie above, but when he came up for the fourth time he had a clear picture of the launch below.

He came up, and clung to the side of the boat. Charlie saw the look in his face, and said, 'It is?'

Furse nodded. 'Yes. We're lucky.'

He pulled himself aboard and sat breathing heavily. After a while, he said, 'There is too much water, and the current's too strong yet. I can manage it at dead slack water. That's an hour from now—'

'OK, sir. We go ashore now and have a bottle of beer I bring with me from Hellevoetsluis.'

They tied a can to the end of the anchor warp and dropped it over to mark the wreck, and then went ashore.

Molenaar was in disgrace. His chief had not said so, but the way he spoke and acted implied it clearly. They were sitting in the *wachtmeester*'s office in Hellevoetsluis which Molenaar had taken over in order to direct the search for Furse. His chief had come down by car from Rotterdam and Molenaar had just made his report.

Molenaar felt that everything was against him. He had not had time to shave or change his trousers which had dried on him. He felt dirty and irritable, but dared not show his feelings. Once or twice while he had been speaking he had got the impression that his chief was enjoying his ruffled state. At the moment he stood by the window, rocking gently on his heels, his hands clasped behind his back.

Molenaar watched him anxiously. From the docks came the rattle and screech of a winch working. It was hot and stuffy in the room, and it wanted dusting. Molenaar made a mental note to see that something was said to the *wachtmeester* about it.

His chief turned slowly and said carefully, 'The Bank is going to be very annoyed . . . So many people are going to be annoyed. It is unfortunate. His boat you say was found at Willemstadt?'

'Just above, sir. Every place along the river has been warned to keep an eye open for him. All the local police know. We shall find him. I've done everything I can think of.'

The chief shrugged his shoulders. 'I don't doubt it. However, if he escaped once, he can do it again. If he came back, maybe it was only to pick up the stones and go. Once out of this country we have no hold on him. No proof.'

'There's his boat. The Customs people brought it in this morning.'

'So. But, after a lot of delay, it will have to go back. Technically he has not even committed an offence. We requested him to go, but he came back. Oh, perhaps we could bring up some minor offence, obstructing you . . . But what does all that amount to? Nothing. If he gets away with the Bank's property we shall never know. At this moment things may be very awkward for him, but they are also awkward for us. If we can catch him, we can make sure this time that he goes under order and never comes back, and that he takes nothing with him. What about his friends, Ponz and Rohner?'

'Charlie Ponz went back to Rotterdam last night. Rohner is still here in his cruiser.'

'I see. Well, Furse isn't likely to be coming here. You'd better get the Customs people to take you down to Willemstadt and see what you can find down there. I'll stay here in case anything comes in. This is all very troublesome, Molenaar. We can only hope he shows his nose somewhere and gives us a chance . . .'

'Yes, sir.'

When Molenaar had gone, his chief still stood by the window. Molenaar, he was thinking, was a good man, but not brilliant. He began to go over in his mind all the details of the various reports which had come to him from Molenaar. Furse had been twice to Hellevoetsluis, the stones had been taken from the Bank at Dordrecht . . . He stood there a long time in thought. Then he took his hat and walked down to the harbour.

The *Arletta* had been towed in that morning by the Customs cutter. He went aboard and began to look around. It was some time before his attention became concentrated on the chart rack. An hour later he was sitting at the cabin table with Chart 192 before him examining it very closely for pencil and other marks.

They had finished the beer which Charlie had brought with him. It wanted half an hour to dead low water. Furse, who was lying in the shade of the last of the poplars, rolled over and sat up. Charlie lay beside him, a collapsed, untidy figure, his linen trousers wrinkled up to show a patch of hairy leg above his socks.

'Time we went.'

There was a touch of impatience in Furse's voice, and he knew that all the time since they had left the water he had been unable to relax as Charlie seemed to have done. He wanted to be back, to have this job finished. Maybe, he thought, Charlie was not as relaxed as he looked. It was an odd thing about Charlie, the way his sad, impertinent manner hid all trace of his real feelings.

A dark shape swept across the glittering stretch of water at the mouth of the cut. A small skiff came up the smooth run of water to them. Furse saw the turn of a head, the glint of sunlight quiver along the rising blades of the oars, and heard the friendly grumble of disturbed water washing away from the bows.

He sat there very still, as though in this moment immobility were his only defence. The reflection of the trees in the water was shattered, danced madly in a kaleidoscope of colour and then raggedly reformed as the skiff drove forward with a last stroke of the oars and grounded alongside their own boat. He heard Charlie stir beside him, but he kept his eyes on the boat. Beyond it on the far side of the cut was a great bush overgrown with a riot of wild convolvulus, the white trumpet flowers cascading towards the water. Somewhere up the cut Beukleman's ducks were calling and protesting amongst themselves as they fed. Constanta Straatsma got out of the skiff and came slowly towards them.

She faced Furse and said, 'I want to talk to you alone.' Her voice was even but only she knew the effort it was costing her to keep her nervousness from it. She stood there in a crumpled grey flannel skirt, a white blouse showing between the loose edges of a canvas windbreaker, the dark hair short and disarrayed above the wide brow, the whole of her body set in a taut, stubborn stance.

Charlie said suddenly, half turning to Furse, 'This is your problem, captain. You want my advice? Damn me – cut her throat and bury her.'

'Shut up, Charlie!' He spoke fiercely and for the moment he was confused. All he knew was that he didn't want her here.

'I'd like to talk to you alone,' Constanta repeated firmly.

Charlie moved away from them and over his shoulder he growled, 'I don't feel so happy in this kind of conversation, anyway. When I come back, captain, I hope you know what is to be done.' He moved off into the trees towards the house and as he went he began to whistle gently, a sad little shrilling of sound, resigned and pathetic.

'How did you know we were out here?'

'Does it matter?'

That morning early, unable to sleep, she had walked a mile down the river bank and below the town had seen Charlie go by in midstream. Knowing he was supposed to be in Rotterdam her curiosity had been roused. From the high river wall she had watched him through her glasses, seen him round the seaward end of Krabbensplaat and had waited for him to appear in the gap between that island and Tien Gemeten. He never had appeared. When the *Arletta* had been brought in it had not been hard to guess what might be happening. After that, because of her feeling for Furse, she had known that she must see him. She had waited her moment to get away unobtrusively. She said now:

'You don't have to worry. No one knows I've come here.'

'Why have you come?'

'Because I love you and because I don't want you to be a fool. You don't have to tell me what you're doing. I know.'

'What do you know?'

'Everything. It was I who financed Sluiter.'

'You!' He stared at her in surprise. 'But I had no idea . . .'

146

'I know you took Sluiter's papers,' she went on vigorously. 'I know what you're hoping to find out there.' Her head jerked towards the river.

Furse thought he caught a note of contempt in her voice and answered bitterly :

'I suppose you think I murdered Sluiter?'

'No, you didn't do that. But you robbed him, when he was dead!'

'Maybe.' The truth cut into him, rousing him to anger. 'Maybe I am a thief. But what about you and Sluiter. You were going to rob the Bank.'

Constanta stared at him in amazement. Then she answered quietly, 'You're wrong. We were going to claim the reward offered for finding the stones.'

'Reward?'

'Yes.'

Furse was silent. He looked away from her, and Constanta hated herself for the humiliation she had caused him. She went on gently, 'Can't you see that there's only one thing for you to do if you ever want any peace or a decent life after this. You've got to give this up and go to Molenaar.'

'Like hell!' It was his pride speaking.

'You know I'm right. You might get away with the stones and Charlie could pass them – but the money would never do you any good.'

'I'm in this, and I'm staying in it.'

'I don't believe it. You're not being honest.' She put her hand on his arm. 'The day we went to Willemsdorp you were honest. When you saw I loved you, you turned away from me because of this thing. I didn't understand at first. But I understand now. If you get the money, you'll spend the rest of your life turning away from people and things ... Don't be an idiot. You know I'm right.'

He was silent. At this moment he had no words for her. All the trouble was now in the open between them. There was no question of any compromise. He loved her – but if there was to be any future for that love he had to abandon all he had worked for, throw overboard all the plans he had made for Jimmy and himself. Was it worth that? Even putting the question to himself made him feel mercenary, unclean— But what the hell! What was love anyway? At this moment it seemed vital. But in a year, two years . . .? Some demon forced him to lacerate his feelings for her. A man's character was constant. He could give everything up for her now. But later, would the old evil in him reassert itself? Would he have regrets? And, anyway, was it not too late already? The self-torture became almost physical. He moved impatiently and, his voice harsh and agonized, said brusquely, 'There's nothing for you here. I want you to go.'

'You can't mean that.' She put her hand out to him, but he stepped away. 'You're making yourself say that. And there's no need to—' She broke off suddenly, seeing the look on his face.

His eyes were on her hands, held together before her, clenched and pressed together as though she held invisible reins, curbing and straining against a wild, panic-struck force that threatened to run away with her.

He said coldly, 'I want you to go.'

He heard her breath leave her as though she had been struck, and then she turned and he watched her go back along the little path between the poplars, and he was telling himself that it was the only thing. He had had to do it . . . There was no place for her in his life . . . No place at all.

She went down the path, the dappled shadows and lights from the sun through the trees moving over her, and she looked small and insignificant and he could see the creases in the back of her skirt from sitting on the skiff's thwarts and the dirty marks on the elbows of her windbreaker and the dark disorder of her hair. He saw her put out a hand to steady herself against a tree trunk as she dropped down to the little ridge of sand at the side of the cut. The movement of the hand was suddenly so well known to him, so immediate and vivid a part of her, that he almost felt it on his own arm, remembered how her hand had rested on him. He caught the quick surge of a warm anger in himself and against himself . . . and then, suddenly, he was running.

'Constanta!'

She turned, standing by the skiff, as he jumped down the bank and then she came to meet him, her face lifted up, touched with a swift gladness. He caught her and held her against him and the press of her body against him was a comfort he had always wanted, the movement of her hands and her lips against his face, the soft cry of his name in her throat, the only things he had ever wanted.

He had less trouble with Charlie than he had anticipated. When he told him that he was going back to Hellevoetsluis to Molenaar, that he was giving the whole thing up, and that the reward would go to Constanta, Charlie merely shrugged his shoulders, and said : 'When I see the young lady come, I know this must happen. It is a pity, sir. But I don't make no fuss. But I tell you what, sir. Don't go to Molenaar empty-handed.'

Furse took his point. Although the tide had now turned, there was still a chance of getting the stones. No one could doubt his good faith if he came so endowed.

They went out in Charlie's boat, and he dived. The tide had turned almost an hour now and the current was strengthening each moment. He found that the launch was lying almost over on her side and that the cockpit was so full of sand that it came about a foot up the front of the cabin door.

When he came up, Constanta asked, 'Will you be able to do anything?'

'I don't know.'

'Try. It'll make things better with Molenaar . . .' She smiled and he knew the anxiety in her for him. He determined that if he could reach the stones, he would.

He went down and found the cabin door again. He held himself there by the curved handle and then with his free hand got a grip on the cabin top. He pushed hard at the door and felt it give slightly. Then the handle broke away from the wood in his fingers. His feet came up from under him and he was swept away. He came back, thrusting against the tide, and got a fresh grip on the cabin top, digging his nails into the rotten wood. Holding there, his lungs bursting for air, he drew up his feet and pounded against the door. One of his feet broke through a rotten panel. He lost his hold and he was held by the foot while his body was flung backwards. Panic seized him for a moment and he kicked and threshed like a trapped animal. Then the rotten wood crumbled around his trapped foot and he shot to the surface, grabbing at the dinghy anchor line trailing from the boat.

Constanta and Charlie watched him, his shoulders heaving as he breathed deeply, his eyes shut for the moment against the strain of his struggle. He said nothing.

He went down again and this time he got a firmer grip on the cabin top, working his fingers through the rotten wood and gripping the brass runner that protected the edge of the cabin roof. He raised his feet and felt for the solid door timbers, avoiding the thin panels. He drew his legs up and kicked hard. The door gave, swayed beneath his feet and then collapsed inwards as the hinges were drawn from the rotten frame. He hung there for a moment, his body swept half inside the cabin. There was a thundering in his ears and a cascade of white flecks danced before his eyes from the strain of holding his breath. He let go of the cabin top and the tide, running fiercely now, dragged him away.

He came up a few yards beyond the dinghy and had to fight his way back. When he reached it he hung on to the stern, his shoulders heaving, his mouth drawing hungrily at the air. After a while he said, 'I've kicked the door in. I'm going to have one more try, but I think the current will beat me.'

Constanta said, 'Don't try it. You could easily be trapped in the cabin.'

'I'll watch out for that.'

Charlie said nothing.

Furse shook his head and the whip of his hair splattered them with spray. 'One more go and then I'll call it a day.'

He swam a dozen yards up against the tide, drifted for a

moment while he filled his lungs and then slid under, letting the current bear him down on the sunken launch.

'It's too dangerous to play about down there now,' Constanta said it almost to herself as she watched the brown sweep of water. Then she held her own breath as a check on the time he should stay below, knowing that if he were not up shortly after she was forced to breathe again she would go below for him. Charlie was no good. He had already said he could not swim. She watched the waters anxiously and the beat of her heart was loud in her ears, so loud that it covered the quiet approach of a white-painted cabin cruiser that came suddenly down on them from the seaward end of Krabbensplaat.

CHAPTER THIRTEEN

Furse came up about fifteen yards below the boat. He swam back to the dinghy, his eyes half closed in the desperation of physical exhaustion. For a moment down below he had thought he was never going to get up again.

He grabbed the counter of the dinghy, and felt a hand slip under his arm and hold him up. Constanta's face appeared mistily before him and he gave her a wry smile. He hung there, coughing with the salt water in his lungs and slowly his head cleared.

'It's no good,' he said. 'We might just as well pack up—' His words died away. He saw Constanta's face, grave, and about her lips a slight tremble that might have meant nearness to tears or anger. Behind her Charlie was watching him, too. The round boyish face was lax, the corners of the mouth drooping lugubriously.

'What's the matter with you two?' he asked. Before they could reply, he became conscious of a gentle thudding in the air. He turned his head and saw, close to the bows of the dinghy, the clumsy form of a cruiser. Standing on deck was Rohner. His surprise was so great that for a moment he stared stupidly at the man. Then, the full import of what had happened coming to him, a surge of desperation took him. He swung forward along the dinghy side, impelled by a furious desire to get at Rohner, a primitive instinct to throw himself against the forces which represented calamity and misfortune.

Something of what was in his mind became clear to Constanta. With a quick movement she seized his arm.

'Don't – you wouldn't have a chance !' she cried.

From the deck of the cruiser Rohner's voice followed hers, 'No, you wouldn't have a chance, Mr Furse.'

Rohner lifted the revolver which he held in his hand. 'You must accept the inevitable. I always told you I would come in when the moment was right – but this time there's no partnership.'

'How the hell did you get here?' Furse asked. His blind impulse to get at Rohner was gone now. He had to think carefully, match the man with his own cunning.

Rohner shrugged his shoulders and gave no answer. Behind him stood Elsa, leaning slightly back on a boat hook which had been crooked over the far counter of the dinghy. At the wheel was Pieter in a loose, highly decorated American shirt and in the bows in his stiff blue suit but with an open collar stood Anselm Dekker. He, too, held a revolver in his hand, and, when Furse caught his eye, he turned away, a faint shade of embarrassment touching his face.

'Trouble,' said Charlie apologetically to Furse, the lines of his face turned down miserably. 'He was on us before we could do anything.'

Rohner gave a little wave of his revolver and said pleasantly, 'Get in the boat and put your clothes on, Mr Furse.'

Furse hesitated for a moment. Rohner's smile was that of a man who stood on top of the world and meant to stay there.

'I'm surprised you took the risk of coming back,' he went on. 'But I'm glad you did. Get in the boat. If all three of you behave there won't be any trouble for you.'

Furse went round to the stern and hauled himself aboard. He was cursing himself for not having given more thought to Rohner.

'How the hell did you find us?' he asked bitterly.

Rohner shrugged his shoulders. 'I have a better information service than the police. Get dressed.'

'It's a nice body,' Elsa said as Furse began to rub himself down, 'but not so beautiful or so brown as Pieter's.' She laughed. She, too, was sharing Rohner's exhilaration.

Furse looked at Constanta and saw that she was more puzzled than afraid. 'For the moment,' he said, 'just do as they say. They'll know that it isn't out of respect for their characters, but because of the guns in their hands.'

'Mr Furse sounds disappointed,' said Rohner. 'Charlie –

throw the painter aboard. We'll tow you in. You can leave the mooring can where it is. I presume it marks the position of Captain Maserling's launch? What did you find down there, Mr Furse?'

'A lot of sand and water.'

'We'll talk about that later.'

The painter was passed to the launch and the boat hauled close up alongside. Pieter opened up the launch motor and they were towed into the cut where the cruiser was brought alongside the quay.

'Elsa – you and Dekker take Charlie and the girl up to the house and lock them in. There's an old fellow called Beukleman and his wife up there – keep them in as well. Come on—' he motioned to the three in the boat and they climbed up on the deck of the cruiser to pass to the shore. Rohner motioned to the cabin of the cruiser as Furse came up last. 'You go in the cabin.'

Furse did as he was told. After a few moments Rohner followed him with Pieter. Pieter stood at the door while Rohner, revolver in hand, faced Furse across the cabin table.

'You were a fool not to have accepted my offer of a partnership long ago, Furse. We could have cleared up this business before Molenaar ever got round to sending you back.'

'How did you know Beukleman's name?'

'I'm asking the questions. Not you. There's a lot I know which would surprise you . . . Yes, a lot. I am right, am I not, in supposing it was the launch you were after down there?'

'Anything you want to know you can find out for yourself.'

'Oh no. You're going to tell me all you know – otherwise I shall have to turn Pieter on you. It would be a silly thing to make me do. You'd be badly beaten up. Even if you didn't talk I could go and find out all you know for myself in an hour. I can do more than that. Low water's some time after midnight. Pieter can swim and dive like a fish. He can go down and get the stuff. It's more sensible for you to talk.'

Furse was silent. Rohner was quite right. Keeping silent wasn't going to help much. The only comfort he could find in the situation was that by now no one could go down and examine the launch until the next low water. Even if Rohner sent across to the mainland and got a diving outfit right away the current was too strong to use it safely except around low water – and anyway a diving outfit meant risk as well. Time was his only ally at the moment and it seemed that he had a fair amount in hand.

Rohner faced him, and the edge of his teeth bit gently at his lip. 'There's no point in being stubborn, Furse.' He glanced at Pieter who came forward a step.

Furse shrugged his shoulders.

'All right. I'll tell you. The launch is down there. She's lying over on one side, but without a diving suit you can't work on her except just around dead low water. The current's too strong, otherwise.'

'Did you get in the cabin?'

'No. I managed to kick the door in but that was as far as I got before the current became too much for me. You'll never get away with this, Rohner. The moment you leave this place I'm going straight to Molenaar. It means trouble for me, but a lot more for you.'

Rohner shook his head. 'Don't worry about me. There's just a possibility that I may have to fix it that neither you nor any of the others are left in a state to do any talking.'

'You'd be crazy to do anything like that!'

'I don't think it will be necessary. I can be out of this country in a few hours . . . that's all I need. Low tide tonight. Pieter, it looks as though you're going for a swim. If you find you can't do it, we'll send over for a diving outfit and have it here by midday tomorrow. Stay quietly in the house with your friends, Furse, and you won't come to any harm. If you try anything funny there won't be any half-measures. There's too much money in this for me to take any chances.' As he said it the smile was gone and the face which ordinarily was handsome and animated was suddenly thin and mean.

He stood up and backed to the door of the cabin. Furse followed him and he was escorted to the shore.

Furse walked slowly towards the courtyard of the house. There was nothing he could do and no help that could be expected from outside. Molenaar knew nothing of Krabbensplaat. Molenaar might miss Charlie and Rohner, but that wouldn't help him to find them. If Constanta's non-return to her barge that night made Oom Paul and Klara anxious it would be a long time before they went to the police and even then there was nothing to lead anyone to Krabbensplaat. It seemed to him that they could be kept on this island for days without anyone coming there . . . There was going to be trouble, more trouble than anyone except himself realized.

He stopped with his hand on the wrought-iron gate. Behind him he felt Rohner's muzzle press gently into his back.

'You know,' Furse said without turning, 'you might beat the police, you might get clean away and settle down comfortably somewhere – but there's one person who won't take kindly to this. He'll make it his life work to find you.'

Pieter pushed by him and opened the gate and stood waiting for him to pass through. He had a calm, satisfied half-smile on his face and Furse noticed that his nails were beautifully kept. His shirt, which was patterned with green sea-horses and blonde-haired mermaids, was open to show his hard, brown, perfectly modelled chest.

'Charlie, you mean?' It was Rohner and the pressure of the gun forced him forward.

'Yes. He can be a very mean character.'

'Maybe – but I can handle Charlie if he ever finds me.' He laughed again and in the bright sunshine the sound had an ugly ring.

In the hallway of the house they found Elsa and Dekker, and the two Beuklemans with Constanta and Charlie.

Beukleman came across to Furse.

'Mynheer Furse – what does all this mean? All these people?' His old face was worried and his eyes blinked nervously. His wife moved behind him like a shadow, her face puzzled and angry.

Furse put a hand on his arm.

'I'm sorry about it. I'll explain later. But for the time being you must do what these people tell you.' He felt like a father calming a child and at the same time he was angry that Rohner should have brought this unpleasantness into the Beuklemans' lives. Not only Rohner, he thought, but he himself had helped . . .

'But they tell me I cannot go out of the house.'

'That's true.'

'But what about my herd? It is almost milking time. If they are not milked it will be very bad for them.'

Furse saw the old man's lower lip tremble gently.

'What does he expect us to do – milk them for him?' Elsa moved towards the door as she spoke and Furse saw that she was carrying the telephone under her arm.

'Surely you can let him milk his cows?' Furse looked at Rohner. 'He thinks the world of his Friesians.'

'Have him wandering loose all over the island? Think again, Furse.'

'They're only in the pasture at the side of the house. Dekker can drive them into the yard and he can milk them there.' Somehow his own troubles had vanished, and it had become absurdly important that he gained this concession for Beukleman.

'What, me milk them?' Dekker's voice sounded genuinely alarmed.

'Damn it!' said Furse. 'You're taking over his house, Rohner. It's the least you can do. If the old man milks them out there, you can keep an eye on him.'

Rohner hesitated for a while.

'Stop fussing around about the old fellow,' said Elsa impatiently. 'Can't you see that our friend here is hoping he can make something from it?'

Rohner shrugged his shoulders. 'I don't know . . . He can't do any harm. All right, Furse. When Dekker has driven the cows in, he can come out. But the rest of you keep to the house. You're here until tomorrow and if you're wise you won't try to get out.'

They were left alone in the hallway, Constanta, Charlie, Furse and the two Beuklemans. The key turned in the great doorway.

Charlie sat down on one of the stiff, tapestried chairs and lit a cigarette. He looked ruffled and dispirited as he said :

'It always happens, sir. You try to be virtuous – and something bad like this happens. For me, it's better to stick to wrong-doing then I keep my eyes open always. Not like just now.'

Charlie went off to the kitchen.

'Where's he going?' asked Beukleman's wife. No one answered her and after a while Charlie came back. He made a hopeless gesture and said to Furse :

'Our friend Elsa has locked the door at the back. All the windows on the ground floor are barred as though it were a prison. Damn me, it is a prison, unless, sir, you feel like jumping from the second floor and risk being shot. Anselm Dekker is a good shot. So is Rohner. Pieter and Elsa may not be so good, but that don't make me feel any happier.'

'Four of them – that means they can have two on duty all night. At least we shall get more sleep than they do,' said Constanta.

'I wrote Rohner off too easily,' Furse said it bitterly.

Charlie shook his head. 'It was not your fault, captain.'

Beukleman's wife moved towards the kitchen and her voice echoed harshly in the great room :

'Some time maybe you will be good enough to explain this intrusion. In the meantime I will prepare some supper. Also—' she glanced at Charlie as she passed him '—you will be good enough to be careful with your cigarette ash.'

When she was gone Beukleman gave Furse a little smile.

'Thank you, sir, about the cows. Do not be too upset about my wife. This is her house. She does not care to see it turned into a prison.'

'Neither do I – but unfortunately we have no choice.'

From the window at the head of the staircase, Furse and

Constanta watched Dekker driving the cows in from the pasture, a stiff awkward figure, obviously embarrassed by the rôle of farm-hand. He waved his arms and shouted and the animals turned and stared at him curiously. It was a long while before he could get them to move.

Furse stood watching, his arm round Constanta's shoulder. The cows padded into the yard and, when they were all in, Rohner unlocked the great door and called Beukleman out. Furse watched him go slowly across the yard to the dairy and fetch his milking stool and his pails. He sat down alongside Kadza and began to milk her. Dekker squatted on the yard gate by the pasture, his revolver resting in his lap. Pieter lay along the top of the brick wall by the wrought-iron gate and Furse noticed that since leaving the house he had been provided with a shot-gun. Rohner disappeared towards the back of the house and Elsa went down to the launch. It was an odd scene, Beukleman milking placidly, going from cow to cow, while the two armed men watched him.

'This morning,' said Constanta, 'I thought I was never going to see you again.' She put her hand up and rested it on his which was on her shoulder.

He turned her round and held her from him, his hands in hers, looking at her and his face was thoughtful, a little strained.

He said evenly, 'You do mean it still, don't you? No matter what I am, what I meant to do – it makes no difference?'

'None.'

She smiled at him and her dark eyes were alive with quick points of light.

He bent forward and kissed her quickly.

'You're crazy. All you get is me. There won't be any reward money from the Bank. Damn Rohner. How did he find us?'

'Rohner hasn't succeeded yet. The police may find us. Maybe we can do something.'

Furse shook his head. 'I don't see what we can do.'

'Neither do I, sir.' It was Charlie who had come up behind them. 'Rohner is a very competent person. Very competent and very ruthless. He don't have any respect for other people's health.' He gave a little bow to Constanta. 'Congratulations. You will have lots of headaches. For me, I am married once, but there is nothing in it for a man of my temperament.'

Before supper Furse went all round the house. On the ground floor all the windows were barred, in the front with the graceful, swan-necked curved ironwork which swept back to within a few inches of the top of the window embrasures, and at the back with a plain grille of bars not more than three inches apart. The only ways out were through the hall door and the door at the end of a corridor beyond the kitchen. Both of them were locked. Outside the front sat Dekker, while in the rear Rohner had made himself comfortable against a low wall on a pile of hay he had dragged out from one of the barns. The lowest of the windows on the first floor was thirty feet from the ground. Rohner, Furse guessed, was taking the early evening shift. The watch around midnight would be taken by Elsa and Dekker while Rohner and Pieter worked on the sunken launch.

Returning to the front of the house he opened the window at the head of the staircase and called down to Dekker :

'What's it worth to you to toss up your gun and the key of the front door?'

Dekker raised his head.

'My life.'

Dekker slipped off the gate, the yard had long been cleared of the cows, and walked across until he stood under the window.

'Rohner will ditch you once he leaves here.'

Dekker lifted the revolver. 'Not as long as I have this. You're wasting your time. I don't intend to do anything for you. Now you will please shut the window. It is forbidden for the prisoners to talk to their guards.'

'There are lots of other prison regulations you'll get to know in good time.' Furse drew the window down. He stood there, watching Dekker go back to his perch on the gate. The light was going and over the tops of the trees by the cut he could see a heavy bank of cloud forming ponderously in the west. The wind had gone round and it looked as though the night might bring rain. He hoped so, not because it would be any help to him, but because it would at least make their guards uncomfortable.

In the hall he found Charlie sitting at the long refectory table playing patience. Through the open doorway into the kitchen he could hear Constanta talking to Beukleman's wife. The sound of Constanta's voice made him thoughtful. He'd been more fortunate than he deserved to be. It was up to him now to see he never disappointed her. He felt himself suddenly impatient of the present, eager to be free to start a new life with her and Jimmy, to show her she had made no mistake about him.

Charlie looked up at him and it was some time before he spoke. His eyes on Furse were very still and his lips were pursed, pouting a little like a boy who contemplates some impudence prompted by frustration. Then, when he spoke, Furse had the feeling that his words were far from his thoughts.

'She will make a good wife, just as now she makes a good mayonnaise, captain. You understand that about a woman? Not me. With all this sitting over her she makes the mayonnaise for supper. What are you going to do about Rohner, sir?'

'What can I do?'

'That don't sound like you. In Italy it was worse than this, but the only thing you worry about is will the wine hold out.'

'Things were different then.'

'So? I have a feeling you don't want to do anything about Rohner. I am asking myself why when you talk to Dekker just now and he comes under the window you don't drop onto his shoulders. You get his gun and everything is different.'

'I didn't think of it.'

'It makes me curious. There is something here I don't understand, sir. It is not good to have mysteries between old friends.' He lowered his eyes from Furse's face and carefully put a queen of spades on a king of diamonds.

'Supper's ready.' Constanta had come into the hall. She

waited for Furse as he went towards the kitchen and put her hand on his arm. 'The Beuklemans want to know what all this is about. We should tell them. Or rather you should tell them, then you needn't go into unnecessary details.'

'Thinking of my reputation?'

'Why not? It belongs to me as well now.'

Beukleman's wife, pursuing her philosophy that men in trouble need food, had not stinted the meal. A wide, pink-bowled oil lamp hanging from the ceiling shed a soft, warm glow over the table. There was a rich *fermière* soup, a great plate of cold ham and cold duck with a bowl of salad for which Constanta had prepared the mayonnaise. After he had finished his soup, Furse looked up at Beukleman. He was sitting at the head of the table. A black velvet jacket had taken the place of his crinkled leather waistcoat and he wore a spotless linen shirt with two tiny bands of lace running down the front of it. The black and white gave a dignified almost delicate air of fragility to his face which was in odd contrast to the lean, work-browned hands. His wife sat close to him, neat, compact, lowering her head a little at times to look through her glasses at her guests' plates. She missed nothing, said little and her expression was taut, a suggestion of fierce tenderness in it whenever she turned to her husband.

'Have you ever,' asked Furse, 'heard of Kapitan Walter Maserling?'

Beukleman raised his head slowly. He looked first at Furse and then at his wife and Furse saw her lips tighten. She gave a little nod towards her husband.

'Yes, mynheer. I have.'

'He was in this house during the war?'

'Yes, mynheer. He was here for three days, very ill. For a time even he was delirious. Then he left us suddenly. I have told you before that we gave shelter to anyone who came. A sick man has no nationality.'

'I've no quarrel with that. I mention him because it is necessary in order to explain why there is this trouble, trouble which we have brought on you and for which I apologize now.'

Beukleman nodded and then said, 'So long as I can milk my cows . . . that is the chief thing. But you must not think I am not angry. Both mother and I are very angry, but we do not show it. Angry, not with you, but those people out there. But I do not understand what they have to do with this German captain?'

'You will.'

Furse began to explain. He went into no unnecessary details as Constanta called them, but gave the broad outline of the mission which Maserling had been carrying out.

'Mr Ponz and I had come here with Miss Straatsma to recover the Bank's property. But unfortunately our friend Rohner outside had become aware of our intentions. He is going to take it for himself. A quarter of a million pounds is a sum which would tempt any man.'

'It is enough money to make Rohner very careless how he handles people if they get in his way,' Charlie said, and then, with a glance across at Constanta, went on, 'You are going to be unlucky over the reward, miss. Once Rohner gets his hands on that stuff he'll be away so clean as a whistle. He knows how to disappear.'

Furse looked around the table at them. Constanta gave him a smile. She had a reserve of confidence which was illogical but unshakable. It was a quality which at this moment he could not share. Charlie was cutting a piece of ham into tiny squares and feeding himself with delicate, precise movements which gave away his abstraction. Charlie, he was sure, was miles away, scheming, and plotting how to stop Rohner. There was nothing Charlie could do. The two Beuklemans met his look and he had a sudden unexpected feeling that of everyone present they alone were sharing a presentiment of disaster with him. It was an odd feeling and one which now, he knew, he must bring into the open. They all had to know.

'The real trouble,' Furse said deliberately, 'is that Rohner isn't going to get his hands on the jewels. He's going to be disappointed. And disappointment will make him vicious. You see, the stones are no longer in the sunken launch.'

CHAPTER FOURTEEN

Charlie had a piece of ham halfway to his mouth. His head turned slowly towards Furse and his mouth trembled ridiculously like a child's on the point of tears. Then, his voice unexpectedly high-pitched, he said :

'Damn me, sir. That's what it was? That was what you were hiding, why you didn't jump on Dekker or bother about getting out of the house.'

Furse saw them all staring at him; the Beuklemans stiff and looking like a couple from one of their own oil-paintings in the great hall; Charlie, round-eyed, and Constanta, puzzled, the soft lamp glow throwing a warm shadow across her face.

'But I don't understand.'

Furse put out a hand and touched Constanta's arm, the pleasure from the contact with her warm, brown skin for a second overlaying all the anxiety inside him.

'It's true. There's nothing in the launch cabin but an empty steel deed-box. When I went down the last time I got in easily and there was the box. The lid was open and it was empty.'

'But why didn't you tell us, sir?'

'You know why, Charlie. I came up to find Rohner there. Why should I tell him anything? Time is what we want. And when we got back here I wanted to think the thing over. I had to keep it to myself.'

'You could have been mistaken.'

'No, Constanta. I'm sure of it. Someone got there before us. And when Rohner finds out there's nothing there, he'll think we've double-crossed him. That's the moment when he's going to be very unpleasant, and the moment we've got to avoid.'

No one spoke. Beukleman's wife poured coffee into an array of green cups before her, and her husband mechanically passed them down the table. Outside the wind had freshened and they could hear the sound of it fretting through the tall poplars by the cut. They sat there, the five of them, held in the spreading cone of pink light from the hanging lamp, the great kitchen range squatting like a blue and black monster in the chimney recess, and the piquant aroma of coffee rising about them.

Charlie dusted the lapels of his linen jacket and blew a tiny jet of smoke.

'For me, sir – I will wait until the trouble comes. Blood you cannot get from a stone, and Rohner cannot get out of us what we haven't got. Though he might draw a little blood. What I want to know is – where is all this stuff now? Who was it that got here before us?'

Constanta said, 'I don't see how that helps us. Anyone might have taken them at any time.'

Beukleman put down his coffee cup and drew at a cigar which he had quietly lit. He looked at Constanta and gave her a tired little smile and then he glanced at his wife. She was tight-lipped, tense and the reflection of light on her glasses gave her face a blank, inhuman look. Slowly she nodded.

Beukleman turned back to Constanta and he said quietly, 'Mejuffrouw, I am the one who has taken them, and it was done the day after Kapitan Maserling entered this house.'

It was said so quietly that for a while none of them seemed to realize what had been said. Beukleman sat there, his cigar poised carefully before him, his blue-white face marked with forceful shadows. Slowly he reached out a hand and laid it on his wife's without looking at her.

'Yes, I took them,' he said, and his words now brought them to life.

'You took them?' Furse stared at him, astonished.

'Yes, mynheer – or rather I stole them.'

'Jan!' There was anguish in his wife's voice.

Beukleman turned to her. 'It is the truth, my dear. You know it and now it is better to tell it and have the thing from my mind.'

'Where are they? These shocks – damn me – I don't accommodate them so good.' Charlie stood up, impatient, suddenly animated.

'Let him tell it his own way,' said Furse.

'This is what I shall do, mynheer. But you must be patient with me. You see, this captain I found early one morning at the courtyard gate. He was wounded and ill. In this house he was in bed for three days before he left us. The first day he was delirious and kept talking about the stones. It was not difficult to find the launch. She lay just off the mouth of the cut and at low water high on the sand. I found the box in the cabin and the jewels. I took them. When the tide rose I towed the launch off into deep water where she would always be covered even at low tide. After three days, when the captain was still not really well enough to travel, he took my skiff and went over to the mainland. He did not say one word to me about the stones, and so I knew they did not belong to him.'

'But did you know where the stones came from?' asked Furse.

Beukleman gave a little shake of his head and, while he hesitated, his hand went up and touched his forehead as though to still some unpleasant thought. Then he said, speaking slowly, 'No. When you steal something, it is easier not to know anything about the owner . . . At least, that is what I felt.'

Furse stirred uneasily. The words were an echo of his own feelings, but it was odd to find the same feeling in Beukleman. Nothing, he would have said a little while before, could have ever made the old man a thief.

'Why did you do it?' he asked.

Beukleman drew hard at his cigar and then said, 'Because of my cows. A week before this captain came the Germans had been to the island and had taken away all my herd except Kadza. They took away fifteen years of my life, fifteen years of hard work during which I had built up the herd to be the best in the Netherlands. At the time it made me hard and angry. When I saw the stones I said to myself that I

166

would keep them and, after the war, use them to buy a new herd. But when the time came to turn them into money and buy fresh stock I couldn't do it. Mama and I decided that it was better to work, to use our own money and to start again. One can steal in a moment of weakness, but after that one has to have a hardness inside to use or sell what one has stolen. I found I did not have that. We hid the jewels and they have remained hidden ever since, for we were afraid for our reputation to hand them over to the police and tell the full story. But I am glad now that I can tell it.'

Beukleman's wife turned to Constanta.

'It was I who persuaded Jan in the first place, mejuffrouw. Only I knew what the loss of his cows meant to Jan. After the war I would still have used the stones, but Jan would not let me—'

'That is not so, my dear.'

Constanta said quickly, 'I understand why you did it. I can't even think that you stole them. You have just been their custodian for all these years.'

'You are very kind.'

Charlie got up and walked round the table to the great range. 'Me, I think like Miss Constanta. But all that is past and finished. You still have the jewels on this island?'

Beukleman nodded. 'Yes. They are well hidden. But I will tell you now—'

'No.' Furse's voice was hard, incisive. 'No, Jan – don't tell us anything. As long as they are safe, that's all that matters. We've still got Rohner to deal with and the fewer people who know where they are the safer it is for us. What you don't know not even hard knocks can get out of you.'

Charlie's face clouded for a moment. Then with a shrug of his shoulders, he said, 'Yes, sir. Maybe that is good. When we have dealt with Rohner, then is the time to worry about the stones.'

'But how are we going to deal with Rohner?' Constanta stood up and began to help clear the table with Beukleman's wife.

'At the moment,' said Furse, 'I don't know. The weather

looks as though it's breaking. If there's rain tonight it might stop Pieter from going down. That gives us a little more time.'

'When you can do nothing, it is a good thing to sleep. I shall go to bed,' said Charlie.

The Beuklemans had plenty of sleeping room. Furse and Charlie shared a room at the front of the house which had two single beds and Constanta had a room to herself at the back of the house.

Charlie went off to bed at once and the Beuklemans were not long in following him. Constanta and Furse sat for a while in front of the range, a red glow over them from the open fire front, and after a while there was no need of words. His arm was around her shoulder holding her close to him, his cheek against her hair.

They went upstairs together and, when he had left her, he went to his bedroom. Charlie was sleeping on his back, fully clothed, his mouth open, his arms and legs spread-eagled. Furse stood at the window. It was a dark night and the wind had turned gusty, shaking the glass and splattering sudden squalls of rain across the yard. From the shelter of one of the buildings in the corner of the yard he caught the sudden gleam of a cigarette end and wondered whether it was Dekker or Elsa standing out there. It was nearly eleven o'clock now. Soon, if the weather allowed them, Rohner and Pieter would be going out to the launch. Pieter was going to have an unpleasant time diving in the dark, and a profitless one.

Just before midnight Rohner stood in the shelter of the dairy doorway, his raincoat collar turned up against the scuds of rain, watching the dark face of the house.

As he lounged there a light suddenly appeared in the house. He straightened up, one hand dropping into his coat pocket to feel first his revolver then the key of the main door. Someone was standing by the window at the head of the staircase holding a match. The little flame was moved slowly across the window three times and then disappeared.

Rohner came out of the shelter of the doorway and walked

slowly across the yard, a driving squall of rain beating against his face and lashing against his coat. He went up to the main door and unlocked it. He stood back, his revolver held ready, and gently pushed the door open with his foot. Someone stirred in the darkness and Rohner said quietly:

'What's happened?'

'You'll soon know.'

There was a little chuckle from the darkness and then someone came through the door. Rohner closed and locked it.

It was five o'clock when Furse woke. It was a grey, misty morning with a fine drizzle falling and the wind had dropped. From the window he could see Dekker on duty by the dairy, but the heavy rolls of mist shrouded Rohner's launch, and the tall poplars along the side of the cut were hidden entirely.

Scratching at the stubble on his chin and wondering whether he could borrow a razor from Beukleman he turned back into the room. Charlie's bed was empty. He went downstairs to the kitchen and found the two Beuklemans already there. Mrs Beukleman was lighting the fire and Jan was just slipping into his leather waistcoat.

'Where's Charlie?'

'He is not down yet.'

'He is. At least he's not in his room.'

'Where is he, then?' asked Beukleman.

'I don't know.'

Suddenly Furse turned and hurried from the kitchen. At the head of the stairs he stopped. A movement outside the window caught his eye.

Coming up from the *Yssel* with Rohner was a familiar figure in a linen suit with an old ground-sheet draped over his shoulders. The two of them came through the wrought-iron gate and crossed the yard. As they passed, Charlie looked up and caught sight of Furse standing at the window. He raised a hand in greeting and shook his head sadly. Then he passed on with Rohner into the pasture at the side of the house.

CHAPTER FIFTEEN

The four of them stood at the window at the top of the stairs and watched Rohner and Charlie drive the herd of Friesians into the yard. The beasts came in slowly, swinging their heads, their black and white flanks shining with rain.

Constanta and the Beuklemans had said little since Charlie's desertion had been discovered. Furse was angry with himself for having trusted Charlie when all his experience of the man should have put him on his guard.

'From the moment he came into the house yesterday morning and asked to use the telephone, I didn't like him,' said Mrs Beukleman sharply as she watched the short, caped figure close the pasture gate on the cows.

'So that was how he got in touch with Rohner – when he left us together.' Furse turned to Constanta. 'I'm a damn fool to have let him take me in. The moment you arrived he must have guessed what would happen.'

'They bring the cows in so that I can milk them,' Jan Beukleman said.

'I can't think why they should be bothering to do that,' said Constanta.

'See Kadza – how full she is. It is time I milked.'

Furse ignored Beukleman and pushed open the window.

In the yard below Charlie and Rohner looked up at the sound. Charlie came across to the house, threading his way through the cows awkwardly and stood well away from under the window. He looked up, his round, rain-glistening face contrite and doleful and he made a pathetic little gesture with his hands and shoulders.

'You are angry with me, sir?'

'You're a dirty little double-crossing swine, Charlie.'

'Certainly, captain. It is unfortunately true. But what is a man to do against his own nature? First I think of you and the lovely miss and I say they are my friends. Then I think of all those lovely stones and I say "A man's best friend is himself". Even now, I do not forget you. You come out of the house and join us and we'll see you have your share and get out of the country safely.'

'Go to hell!'

'That is what I think you say. However, we still have a little business to do together. Unfortunately last night you stop Mr Beukleman from saying where the stones are. We should like to know that now.'

'I'll bet you would.'

Charlie turned towards Rohner who came over and joined him. Rohner pulled his revolver from his pocket and jerked his head towards Beukleman.

'You'd better advise him to speak up, Furse. We can do things pleasantly or unpleasantly. It's up to you.'

Constanta drew back from the window, reaching out a hand to Furse. 'Come away, he may shoot.'

'No. He won't dare.' As he spoke Beukleman came up to his side.

'I shall tell you nothing,' he shouted down.

'You will – and quickly!' Rohner swung round and, looking over the herd, picked out Kadza. He went up to the cow and put a hand on the leather bell strap round her neck. He stood there, smiling up at the group at the window, and said evenly, 'Why do you think we've driven these animals in here? Out of kindness, so you can milk them? Think again. I'll give you five minutes to begin telling me where the stones are. If you don't speak I'll put a bullet through Kadza's head. After that, at minute intervals, I'll shoot the rest until you decide to speak.'

Furse heard the old man gasp and saw his hand go out to the window frame to steady himself. And in that moment he knew that any feeling he had ever had for Charlie was utterly gone, this was Charlie's doing. Rohner would never have known how powerful a threat this would be.

'You must tell them. We can't let them do that to you!' cried Constanta.

Jan Beukleman's wife was watching her husband, her

face stiff and grey, her hands held tightly across her waist.

Furse stood looking down at the yard, at Charlie hunched up under his ground-sheet, a drab, evil little figure now, at the slow movement of the restless cattle over the sleek cobbles, and the raincoated figure of Rohner, revolver in one hand and his wrist raised as he timed Beukleman by his watch. It was a bad moment, a moment when everything came back to accuse him. You started in a small way, excusing yourself for an easy transgression, you found a justification for the first lapse and kept your conscience down . . . but eventually you were trapped. And now, not he alone, but all the others were drawn into it to suffer. He suddenly wished that he could be back on the sunny quayside, wished he could have the moment of meeting Sluiter all over again . . . How differently he would act. He'd been a slack, easygoing fool, a cheat and a thief and until this moment had never looked honestly at himself. A fine man, he thought bitterly, a fine father for Jimmy, a fine husband for Constanta . . .

At his side he heard Beukleman begin to speak. His voice was low, trembling with a nervous courage.

'The stones are not mine and I cannot give them away. This is my punishment for the one act which has been a shame to me for so many years . . . My beautiful Kadza . . .' His voice broke in an ugly sob.

Furse reached out for him and took his arm, shaking him. 'You must tell them, Beukleman! Tell them!' He was angry, almost shouting at the old man, feeling himself full of a desperate fury.

Beukleman shook his head. He was looking down at his herd, the sleek black and white animals on whom he had lavished so much love and attention. They moved restlessly under the soft rain.

Furse knew he had no power to make this man speak. This was his punishment, nobler than any he could know for it was self-imposed. Jan Beukleman, too, had been tempted by money, but the old farmer was a better man than he would ever be.

Outside Rohner raised his revolver and shouted:

'You have just under a minute.'

Furse saw Elsa come through the wrought-iron gate and cross the yard to stand at the side of Dekker by the dairy. He saw the tall line of poplars obscured now and again by the drifting veils of mist, and he wondered what he would have done if, instead of the death of Kadza, it had been the burning of the *Arletta* they could have threatened.

Mrs Beukleman came forward and put a hand on her husband's shoulder. His face was set stubbornly but there was a fine tremble to his lips.

'Jan – you must speak.'

'No, mother. I cannot.'

Rohner dropped his wrist and swung round to Kadza. They saw the beast start back from the sudden movement, head lowered for a moment, the great udder swinging. Rohner got a firm grip on the leather collar and brought the revolver against the animal's head just below the ear.

Constanta turned away from the window. She could not watch and she raised her hands to her ears to shut out the sound of the shot.

It was going to happen, Furse told himself. In a few seconds Kadza would be on the ground, her great bulk quivering, the dark, liquid eyes growing dull . . . He shut the picture from him angrily. It was evil and filthy, but it was going to be, and he, God forgive him, had brought it all about out of his own greed and stupidity.

Suddenly Mrs Beukleman leaned out of the window.

'Don't do it!' she shouted angrily. 'Don't do it! I'll tell you where they are, and may God punish you for your wickedness.'

Rohner dropped the hand with the revolver.

'It's time somebody showed some sense up there. Where are they?'

Jan Beukleman tried to pull his wife from the window but she clung there and called out, 'They're buried under a flagstone behind the dairy.' She turned and looked at Furse and

173

Constanta. 'I'm sorry – but I had to do it. I couldn't let them—'

Furse put his arm around her. The stubbornness and passionate strength had suddenly gone from her and she was shaking with nervous relief. 'I'm glad you did it,' he said.

Constanta was with her now. 'You had to do it.'

Rohner at Charlie's side shouted up, 'Send the old fool down to show us. The rest of you stay up there until I've let him out into the yard.'

Slowly Jan Beukleman turned away from the window and went down the stairs, his tall body bent more than ever, his hands limp at his sides.

From the window they watched Jan Beukleman cross the yard with the others. He looked dejected, a spiritless shape, and there was something in the tired movements of the old man that stirred Furse to anger, an anger against himself for having brought trouble and humiliation to the Beuklemans.

At his side, Jan Beukleman's wife looked up at him. He saw her lips tight-pressed against emotion, saw the severe lines of her face as she fought back her anxiety.

Not looking at him now, she said in a voice quiet, yet penetrating with the strain behind it, 'The bad things that happen come from ourselves. But Jan is good. He has always been good. It is from me that the wickedness comes. When he found the stones, it was I who persuaded him they might help us. In his heart he could never accept that. That they were ours by right. After we had built up the herd by our own efforts, he tried again to persuade me to return them . . . We could have told a story about finding them accidentally and, of course, there would have been a reward. But I would not do it. They were ours, I said, one day we might need them. Yes, it is from me that this evil comes . . .'

'Please.' Constanta put her hand on the woman's arm and they began to move down the stairs. Furse followed them.

In the hall, he said, conscious of time slipping by, 'They won't hurt Jan. Don't worry about that. But we've got to do something to stop them from getting away. In an hour they'll be off this island. They'll smash all the boats. Our only way off will be by swimming to Tien Gemeten. It'll be hours before we get the police.'

'They're all armed,' Constanta said.

Furse made an impatient movement. 'I'd take a risk on that – if we could only get out. But with Pieter at the back door and Dekker leaning up against the dairy at the front we have to find another way.'

Mrs Beukleman took off her glasses and began to polish them. She blinked at the two of them and said quietly :

'There is a way out of this house without going through either front or back door, mynheer. Until now neither Jan nor myself had wanted any violence or shooting so we did not mention it.'

Furse stood up. 'Show us,' he said. 'If there is a way out we've got just a chance.'

'From the little harbour at the head of the cut where the boats are there's a large drain that runs right under this house. You can get into it through a trap door in the cellar and where it comes out under the courtyard wall there is an iron grille which, I think, can be lifted off.'

Constanta looked at Furse and he knew they were both thinking the same thing. If there was a way open to them, no matter what the risk, they had to take it.

'Let's see what we can do,' she said quietly.

Furse turned to Beukleman's wife.

'Show us the way,' he said.

Without a word the woman moved across the hall and into the kitchen.

A short flight of steps led off the corridor at the back of the kitchen down to a small cellar. In one corner was a wooden trap door.

'Under there,' said Mrs Beukleman.

Furse lifted the trap door. They could see nothing but there was the sound of slowly running water.

'How deep is it?' he asked.

'About two feet, mynheer, and you understand it is only river water.'

175

Furse smiled. He didn't care what kind of water it was as long as there was a way out. He lowered himself through the trap and felt the water rise above his knees before his feet found the bottom. He moved forward a few paces and was in a narrow tunnel which forced him into a crouching position to clear his head from the roof. Far away he could make out a small circle of daylight.

He heard Constanta drop into the water behind him and he spoke to her over his shoulder. 'Keep your head down and hold onto my jacket.'

They began to move forward slowly. The floor of the drain was muddy and slippery and rough projections from the walls hit against their arms and bodies. A heavy, close odour of mud and rotting vegetation rose about them as they moved. He worked towards the growing patch of daylight, steadying himself against the walls and feeling the water soaking up through his trousers, weighing down the edges of his jacket where it trailed low and when he had to bend to avoid a dip in the roof. Behind him he heard Constanta swearing quietly to herself in Dutch.

After a while the gloom began to give way to daylight and Furse could see the grille across the mouth of the drain. When he came up to it, he found that it was choked with an accumulation of loose seaweed and drift which flowed into the drain with each tide. At low tide, he realized, there would be little more than a trickle of water flowing down the drain.

Constanta was standing alongside him. He saw her face, mud-streaked and her skirt drawn around her legs by the water in it.

'Will it open?' she whispered.

'I think so. It's only dropped into place over staples in the brickwork. You'll have to give me a hand to lift it.'

They stood one at each end of the grille and Furse pulled away the heavy drift from the bottom to lighten it. Through the bars he could see the boats in the small harbour. The outboard motor was still shipped over the stern of Charlie's dinghy. Rohner's launch was at the end of the quay and very close to the mouth of the drain. The drizzle was marking the surface of the water with tiny pocks and long trails of slow-moving mist coiled across the mouth of the cut. Out in the river, he guessed, it would be thicker. It was the kind of wet, misty summer morning when a yachtsman stayed at anchor and busied himself with small jobs about the ship, the kind of morning when people on holiday stayed with their noses pressed against a window pane hoping for the weather to change . . .

'Ready?'

He gave her a nod and they lifted. The grille came up an inch easily and then stuck. Furse strained at it and he heard Constanta give a deep breath as she lifted with him. For a moment the grille was unyielding. Then it moved and there was a long screech of iron against iron as it passed over the staples. They lowered it gently into the water and stood there listening. The noise of grating iron had echoed thunderously in the drain. From outside there was no sound except the gentle passage of rain and an occasional protesting low from the cattle in the yard.

Furse put a hand over Constanta's arm.

'Now listen. Pieter's at the back of the house and won't bother us at first. Dekker's the man we want. He's in front and I'm going after him. You keep close behind me.'

They waded out of the mouth of the drain and climbed up the grass bank that bordered the red brick wall around the courtyard. Keeping close to the wall they worked their way to the wrought-iron gate.

The Friesians were moving slowly about the yard, growing restless from this unusual penning. On the far side of the yard Furse saw Dekker standing by the dairy doorway, his back towards them.

He slipped across the gateway and Constanta followed him. The wall, about six feet high, ran on until it joined one of the sides of the dairy building. At this point Furse stopped.

'I'm going over the top,' he whispered to Constanta. 'I'll work along the dairy wall and then jump Dekker round the corner. I think you'd better go back to the gate. You can watch Dekker from there and give me a signal when to go for him. When you see me get him, you can come across through the gateway. All right?'

Constanta nodded and he put out his hand and touched hers.

'Be careful,' she said gently.

He watched her move back to the gate. When she was in position, he reached for the wall top. He pulled himself up and threw a leg over the wall. A cow standing immediately below him started away and momentarily he feared that the slap of its hooves on the cobbles would betray him. Dekker was out of his sight now, hidden by the angle of the dairy building. From behind the dairy he could hear the scrape of a spade and the murmur of Rohner's voice.

Quietly he crept along the wall until he was a foot from the corner. He stood there pressed against the bricks and glanced across to the wrought-iron gateway. There was no sign of Constanta and he reasoned that she was out of sight because Dekker was now facing her way. He waited and heard the scuffle of Dekker's feet on the cobbles. Then silence. There was the scratch of a match on a box and a trail of cigarette smoke was drawn around the corner by the gentle wind. He stood there, tense, but curiously calm within himself, rubbing the knuckles of one hand against the palm of the other. He heard Dekker cough slightly. Then, glancing towards the gate, he saw Constanta's head. She nodded twice and he knew the moment had come.

He swung round the corner and found Dekker with his back to him. The man heard him coming and half turned. He saw the surprise on Dekker's face, the cigarette dangling from the corner of his half-opened mouth, and a hand swinging up with a revolver in it.

His arm went round the man's neck, forcing it backwards and stilling all sound from him, and at the same time he grabbed the revolver and twisted it from the man's hand. He leaned back, almost dragging Dekker off his feet, and swung the revolver down in a short, vicious stroke, hitting Dekker below the ear. The man crumpled up and his weight nearly brought Furse to the ground. He held him and then backed cautiously through the dairy door and lowered him to the floor. Dekker lay on the ground as though he were asleep. The rain from his cheap coat began to puddle the dry floor and Furse noticed that the sole of his right boot had a hole in it.

He went back to the door and signalled to Constanta. She opened the gateway which swung on well-oiled hinges and came skirting across the yard between the cows that moved ponderously and aimlessly over the cobbles.

A stone slab had been lifted from the ground and Beukleman was scooping up the earth underneath with a long-handled spade. Charlie leant against the dairy wall, his arms crossed under his ground-sheet, the rain making thin rats' tails of his hair. Beyond Beukleman stood Rohner and Elsa looking like mourners who watch the interment of a relative who had been too long a-dying, the thoughts excited by the will to come. Over the wall behind them, which ran back at an angle to the pasture gate, mist and rain came sweeping across the island like smoke rolling from some heath fire.

Charlie was thinking, his mind busy with speculation ... it was a pity he had to bring Rohner into this business, a pity he would have to leave 'Mama' in Rotterdam wondering what had happened to him, but it would have to be done if they were to leave Holland quickly ... and then the stones, they'd lose a fat percentage on them when they were passed ... a pity about Furse – he would have to make him a handsome present some time, but it would have to be done carefully. He watched Beukleman stoop and clear some earth away with his hands. The fingers were long and gnarled and the earth stained them, clinging to them in little clots. Years of hard work, and all he had to show for it was a herd of cows ... and at any time in the last six years he could have walked off with a fortune. It was hard to understand. Yes, sir, it was hard to understand. He pushed himself away from the wall and rubbed the rain out of his eyes. What a life it must be if you spent half your time refereeing a fight between your desires and your conscience. A man might as well be dead because he would never get anything worth having out of life.

Beukleman was lifting a small wooden box out of the hole. Elsa stepped forward and said :

'Here it comes.' Her eyes were bright and she rubbed the tips of her fingers together slowly. Beukleman looked at her and his face was blank.

'It will do you no good,' he said.

'We'll risk that, old man,' Rohner lifted the lid of the box. Inside was a thick sack, folded bulkily over itself and roped together to make a package the size of a small hand-case. Rohner lifted it out and stood holding it with both hands and Charlie came round to his side. Rohner looked at Charlie and smiled, and Charlie returned the smile. At the same time he did two things. He pulled a revolver from his pocket and he slid his hand into Rohner's raincoat pocket and took out the revolver which lay there.

Elsa made a move forward but Charlie dug his revolver into Rohner's side and said, 'Stay where you are, Elsa, or I will blow a hole in him. And don't try to use your revolver. There's nothing in it.'

Rohner stood very still, his face stiff with anger, and he said nothing.

'Very sorry,' said Charlie, 'but the partnership is ended. Now we go quietly across the yard to the launch. If Dekker says anything I will answer. Nobody don't try nothing. I shoot first Rohner and then Dekker.'

Charlie reached out a hand and tucked the sack under his arm. He grinned at Rohner and went on, 'You were going to do the same thing to me, Rohner . . . only you decide to leave it a little later. That is your mistake. When you cheat, cheat early. We go.' He turned a little aside for Rohner to pass him and, as he did so, he saw Furse standing at the corner of the dairy two yards from him with a raised revolver. For a moment Charlie hesitated, not from surprise but because it was Furse standing there, and he knew that his only chance of saving himself was to shoot as he jumped aside from Rohner who was masking his shot. He hesitated because it was Furse, still his friend, and Beukleman, who stood in the small hole, swung his long-handled spade and knocked Charlie's feet from under him.

Charlie fell heavily and a foot was stamped on his revolver wrist holding it down. Furse stood above him, covering Rohner and Elsa.

'Take his gun, Beukleman, and the one in his pocket.'

Beukleman came forward and relieved Charlie of his guns, and then Furse stepped back, releasing him. His eyes on Charlie, Furse said to Constanta, 'Take the sack and get down to Charlie's boat. Go to Tien Gemeten or the mainland and get hold of the police. We'll look after these until they come.'

Constanta picked up the sack.

'You're sure—'

'Yes.' He cut her off curtly. 'You do as I say, and do it quickly.'

It was a new aspect of him to her, harsh, incisive and his whole attention given to the three people whom he had backed up against the dairy wall, 'Watch out for Pieter.'

Beukleman, a gun held awkwardly in his hand, stood beside Furse while Constanta went off. When he judged she was through the yard, Furse motioned the three forward, shepherding them round the corner and into the dairy. They went in quietly, held by the fear of his gun, but he could tell from their manner that each one was alert, waiting for the first false move he made.

There were two small windows in the dairy, each with narrow iron bars. The door was of stout oak, studded with iron rivet heads and fastened on the outside with a thick iron bolt and a padlock.

'Have you got the key for the padlock?' Furse asked Beukleman.

'It's in the house.'

'Go and get it. The house key . . .' Furse made a gesture towards Rohner and slowly the man produced the key of the front door and tossed it to Beukleman. 'Try not to make too much noise. We don't want to disturb Pieter until I've got these safely locked up.'

Beukleman went off across the yard.

Furse stood in the doorway, his back to the yard, and surveyed the three.

Charlie sat down on a milking stool and said, 'Well, sir, how many years do you think I shall get?'

'Two or three.' He did not want to talk to Charlie but somehow it was impossible to ignore him.

'You want to bet on that?'

'No. You're all going to get what's coming to you.'

Elsa made an impatient movement of her shoulders, but her face was white and the thin lips were hard and straight. He knew she was thinking about Sluiter.

Rohner said pleasantly, and the effort to be convincing was heavy in his voice, 'You were a fool to go soft on that girl. You've got the stuff now. Think of it. A fortune for each of us. No trouble about cashing it and no trouble about getting out of the country.'

'You can talk your heads off,' said Furse evenly. He was listening, waiting for the sound of Constanta's outboard motor. Until he heard that he knew he would be uneasy.

On the floor Dekker began to groan and his body stirred as though life were coming back to it painfully.

Elsa said suddenly, her voice uneven and trembling, 'You've got what you want. As soon as the girl is well away . . . please let us go. Let me go . . . you don't have to be vindictive. Handing us over to the police means nothing to you.'

'Maybe you should cry a little. It helps with some men,' said Charlie casually, and went pleasantly on as though this were a conversation between friends, without strain or danger. 'You waste your time, miss. I know this man. I am his best friend and even for me he will do nothing. I do not expect nothing, so I don't disappoint myself. It is hard for you, of course. You will have to answer for Sluiter . . . you and Rohner. But that is the risk you took. For me I don't never take that kind of risk. Prison, yes. I have seen the inside before. In a little while one is comfortable, sometimes happy.'

'Shut up, Charlie, you're talking too much!' Furse snapped, but even as he spoke he realized that Charlie had talked enough to distract his attention vitally.

Pieter's voice behind him said, 'Drop the gun.'

He stood there, poised on the lip of disaster, seeing the sudden exultant change on the three faces before him, knowing that Pieter must have come round by the pasture and missed Beukleman, knowing that Constanta had not yet started her motor, was probably having trouble with it from the rain.

'Drop it!' Something hard was pressed into his back.

'Drop it,' echoed Rohner softly, 'for if you fire at one of us, you'll get a full charge from Pieter in your back.'

Furse dropped the gun, tossing it away into a corner of the dairy. As Rohner had stopped speaking he had caught the quick stutter of Constanta's motor opening up, and he took a chance on Pieter's turning his head at the sound. He swung round, knocking the long barrel of the shotgun from him with a sweep of his hand. His right fist came up and hit Pieter on the chin. The man stumbled backwards. Furse heard Rohner shout. Then, he was running hard for the gateway.

He ran desperately, swinging around the cows in his path, disturbing the beasts so that they tossed their heads and lumbered away from him. There was the roar of a shotgun behind him and he felt the shot whistle past his right side, vicious pieces of lead biting into his arm. It seemed to take him an age to cross the yard to the gate and, as he reached out his hand to swing it open, the other barrel of the gun roared behind him. This time the pellets flew over his head with an angry sound like the passing of a cloud of swarming bees.

He swung open the gate and was through. He could see Constanta standing up in her boat, her hands on the quay about to push off.

He shouted to her and, as he raced towards the water, saw

her move back to the stern, still holding to the quay. Behind him he could hear Charlie and Rohner shouting and the sound of running feet.

He glanced over his shoulder as he crossed the quay and saw them coming out of the gate, saw Constanta waiting in her boat, one hand on the throttle, the other holding to the quay. He leaped aboard. The moment his feet touched the boards she opened up the motor and the boat sped towards the mist-shrouded cut.

'Get down and keep down!' he shouted.

A revolver shot filled the vault of the tree-lined cut with echoes and he heard the bullet slash into the water behind them.

At that moment, away in Hellevoetsluis, it was drizzling, but the rain was showing signs of lifting. Molenaar came out of the post office and turned down the road towards a small café.

He felt dispirited, dissatisfied with himself. His chief was saying little to him, but Molenaar knew that he was expecting a great deal. Furse had made a fool of them. It was up to him to refute that.

He turned into the café and to the woman who came forward he said, 'An Englishman came in here inquiring for a man called Vliegen . . .' He heard himself go through the parrot routine, knowing and finally convinced that he would get nothing of importance from her, and heard the woman reply, 'No. I can't help. Any more than I could help him.'

Molenaar went out. An old man wearing a suit of crumpled corduroy and with gold ear-rings bright against his leathery face stirred in the shelter of the doorway. In a reedy voice, he said, 'Heard what you were asking in there. Looking for Vliegen, eh?'

'Yes. Do you know where he is?'

The man nodded.

'Yes. Take you to him now for twenty guilders. That's what the Englishman paid.'

Hope trembled suddenly in Molenaar.

'Take me to him. Yes, yes . . . you shall have your twenty guilders.'

'Sure? No matter what?'

'Yes.' Impatience harshened Molenaar's voice. 'No matter what.'

CHAPTER SIXTEEN

They lay out in mid-stream, somewhere off Krabbensplaat. Furse had cut the motor the moment he had heard the cruiser come out of the channel after them. The sound of their own staccato engine beating through the mist would have made it easy to place their position. They lay there, drifting on the last of the coming tide. Already the current had slackened.

There was a wind getting up which had begun to tear and thrust at the mist, and the rain had stopped. Sometimes they could see the water for twenty yards around them.

Then their world narrowed to an orbit of a few yards. Long gulfs and corridors suddenly opened up before them, and overhead there was a steady lightening as the sun fought against the high pall of mist and cloud. In another hour it would be a clear, fine day. Every moment the breaks and vistas in the mist changed and eddied. They were lost in a world of dull gossamer curtains that swayed and shifted with every draught, broke and parted, closed and swept in on them with a swiftness which was confusing.

If they were caught out in the river they were helpless. Rohner and Charlie could overhaul them and, if they threw the stones overboard, they would only invite a savage ramming which would probably kill them both. Beukleman and his wife were all right. They were in the house, armed, and no one would bother with them. But here . . . there was nothing to save them but guile.

'They're coming closer,' whispered Constanta and she raised her head, listening as they lay in the bottom of the boat. From out of the mist came the sudden roar of the cruiser. It seemed to be bearing straight down upon them. Then, with a sudden *diminuendo* it swung away and was abruptly muted by the mist and distance. A little later it was back again and this time Furse fancied he caught a glimpse of a dark shape tearing through the mist over their port bow. When it was gone he said: 'They're beating around in a circle hoping to pick us up.'

'What are we going to do?'

'Drift. It's the only thing we can do. The moment we open up they'll hear us. When we've drifted far enough from them we'll take a chance on it and try and hit Tien Gemeten. Trouble is, I'm beginning to lose my bearings in the mist.'

They were silent for a while and in that time the cruiser came back, circling round them, the echo of its engine reverberating harshly from the mist and water.

Suddenly Constanta said, 'I love you.'

Furse lifted her hand and kissed it. 'I love you. I hope Jimmy approves of you – otherwise it will be the first disagreement we've ever had.'

'Do you think he will?'

'He's got his father's good taste.'

'Here they come again.'

The cruiser beat by them and this time, although they could not see it, the wash from its passage set the small boat rocking.

It was gone and silence settled down over the water. They drifted. They lay there, his hand in hers and he could feel her shivering as the cold from her wet clothes struck into her. The silence was eaten into slowly by other noises, the intermittent slap of water against the boat, a distant sound of a clock striking and the slow, melancholy calling of a cow. Once there was a swift, hissing beat of wings and a blackbacked gull came sheering through the mist, stalled above them and then side-slipped away into the oblivion of coiling vapour. But there was no returning sound of the launch. Furse looked at his watch. It was ten minutes since they had last heard it. He sat up and, as he did so, he felt the wind freshen against his face. A clump of loose seaweed drifted by the boat and he fixed the line of the current by it.

'Now.'

He wound the line round the fly-wheel of the motor and gave it a jerk. The engine choked, hesitated, and then burst into life. He put the tiller over and they were heading for the shore of the island of Tien Gemeten, or where he judged it might be. On Tien Gemeten were people, houses, a telephone and safety.

The sound of their motor beat back to them from the thinning walls of mist. Furse was careless of the noise they made now. All he wanted was speed and to get ashore, but as they drove forward he was listening for the sound of the cruiser. Rohner and Charlie might have stopped their motor to wait, drifting until they heard him open up.

The seconds passed and he began to hope that they had escaped the cruiser. Then, away on their port bow, he heard the sudden burst of a motor.

'They're after us !'

He pushed Constanta flat in the boat. There was nothing they could do now except keep going.

He heard the cruiser circle questingly behind them, and then the noise rose to an angry beathing roar and, glancing back, he saw a large shape swing out of the mist across their stern. For a moment he caught the silhouettes of three figures. He swung the boat away at an angle, and the shape was lost. But he heard the shout of voices and knew he had been seen. Zigzagging, but keeping his course, he held the boat on, praying that he might hit Tien Gemeten. If they missed the island and had to make the run for the mainland then they would almost certainly be caught.

The cruiser came sweeping down behind them, breaking out of the mist like some furious leviathan. He saw a figure run towards the bows, saw an arm raised and then, as it was almost up with them, he slammed over the tiller and sheered away sharply. The boat heeled and water for a moment lapped over the gunwale. The cruiser slid by them and disappeared. He heard the note of its motor change, die, then rise angrily and he knew it was coming back. This time, he thought, there would be no escape. They would hold their speed down and manoeuvre with him.

He heard it coming nearer and nearer and he saw Constanta's head turned, her eyes on him. Then, as the sound seemed almost on top of them, the mist before the bows of the boat shifted, eddied in a wanton turn of the wind and momentarily he saw, not five yards from them, the edge of a narrow run of sand and reeds. Beyond it was the rise of a small embankment and, shadowy sentinels beyond the bank, the still forms of a row of pollarded willows.

He shouted, 'It's Tien Gemeten. When we hit the sand run for it and keep on running!'

The mist swept down on them again and the boat slid with a long rasping sound on to the sand. Behind them the launch throttled down suddenly. It hit the sand a few yards from them. He heard Charlie shout, but he took no notice as he leapt overboard and turned to help Constanta. He picked up the sack of jewels and ran with her over the soft sand.

There was a revolver shot and the mist reverberated with angry echoes. He saw the sand kick up at his face.

They raced up the embankment towards the willows. A muddy track ran away from the trees across a flatness of ploughed field. He pushed the sack into Constanta's arms and said urgently:

'Keep on running until you meet someone. I'm staying to look after Rohner.'

She ran on, swallowed by the mist at once, and he slid behind the first willow tree. He leaned against it panting, hearing someone coming across the sand to the embankment. A figure appeared at the top of the bank and he saw that it was Rohner. Charlie, he guessed, had stayed on the launch. They had to have someone there to keep it from drifting away.

Rohner came running across the grass towards the track and Furse saw the ugly blackness of the revolver in his hand. The man came swinging past the tree and, as he did so, Furse jumped out. His arms went round his waist and the full force of his body took them sprawling to the ground. Rohner's fingers around the revolver moved convulsively and the weapon was fired. The noise seemed to split inside Furse's head and he felt the flame from the muzzle scorch his face. He reached out savagely and caught Rohner's wrist and they twisted and struggled, turning over and over on the wet grass. Rohner was wiry and desperate, cursing to himself in French as he fought, but there was an angry pulse in Furse now which found satisfaction in fighting. He took Rohner's blows without feeling, and his hand and arm flexed inexorably as he wrenched Rohner's wrist backwards and, at the same time, drove his free hand, fist clenched, into the man's body. Knees and feet thrusting at the ground for purchase they were for a while a couple of animals absorbed in their struggle. Then, Furse felt the other's wrist collapse and the fighting body under him go limp. He grabbed the revolver and raised himself to his knees. Rohner tried to draw himself away. Furse hit him with the revolver and Rohner dropped backwards.

Furse jumped to his feet, revolver in hand, and saw Elsa standing at the top of the embankment. He went towards her and she turned and ran.

He stood on the embankment and watched Elsa ploughing her way awkwardly across the stretch of sand. And now the wind was suddenly freshening, tearing great swathes of mist away. A shaft of sunlight broke through, turning the dull sand to bright gold and the brown waters of the river to a polished jade. He saw the cruiser, nosed into the sand, and Charlie at the wheel watching Elsa struggling towards it. Charlie raised an arm to him in greeting, and the next moment the motor had opened up and the water at the cruiser's stern was a spume of white froth.

The cruiser backed, swung round and with a great bow wave moved away down the river, towards the sea, towards whatever sanctuary Charlie had arranged for himself. As the cruiser disappeared Furse heard the sound of another motor. A Customs launch came out of the last of the mist, heading towards the shore. Furse saw the familiar figure of Molenaar in the bows, and beside him another man, Molenaar's chief.

The launch swept in to the sands, towards Elsa who waited there, a slight, lonely figure.

Furse turned back towards Rohner. As he moved the mist was lifting off the face of the island and he heard the clink of harness. Slowly up the muddy track came a cart with a man leading the horses. Spread out on either side of the cart were four men and with them came Constanta, muddy and bedraggled, her wet skirt clamped about her legs, her arms still clasping the corded sack and a smile on her face as she saw him there, waiting for her.

Victor Canning

Acclaimed as 'one of the finest thriller writers in the world'.

QUEEN'S PAWN   30p

'Beautifully engineered plot, hair-trigger suspense, set-piece climactic excitement aboard QE2: typically compulsive Canning' – THE SCOTSMAN

THE SCORPIO LETTERS   30p

'Crisp thriller . . . the mysterious blackmailer Scorpio is excitingly and violently unmasked' – DAILY EXPRESS

THE WHIP HAND   30p

'An excellent book for any spy fans . . . Canning plays out another tense, fast-moving tale. Rex Carter, private detective, follows a beautiful girl from Brighton to the Continent and into a spider's web of danger and intrigue' – EVENING STANDARD

THE MELTING MAN   30p

'Few more macabre settings for a climax could be imagined than the private waxworks of a mountain chateau . . . Crisp, polished and as tense as they come' – BRISTOL EVENING NEWS
and

MR FINCHLEY DISCOVERS HIS ENGLAND   35p

THE GREAT AFFAIR   35p

These and other PAN Books are obtainable from all booksellers and newsagents. If you have any difficulty please send purchase price plus 7p postage to PO Box 11, Falmouth, Cornwall.

While every effort is made to keep prices low it is sometimes necessary to increase prices at short notice. PAN Books reserve the right to show new retail prices on covers which may differ from those advertised in the text or elsewhere.